PENGUIN BOOKS
MAHARANI

Ruskin Bond is the acclaimed author of over five hundred novellas, stories, essays and poems, all of which has established him as one of India's most beloved writers. His most recent works are *Secrets* and *Susanna's Seven Husbands* which was turned into the film *Saat Khoon Maaf*. He was awarded the Sahitya Akademi Award in 1993 and the Padma Shri in 1999.

Also by Ruskin Bond

Fiction
The Room on the Roof & Vagrants in the Valley
The Night Train at Deoli and Other Stories
Time Stops at Shamli and Other Stories
Our Trees Still Grow in Dehra
A Season of Ghosts
When Darkness Falls and Other Stories
A Flight of Pigeons
Delhi Is Not Far
A Face in the Dark and Other Hauntings
The Sensualist
A Handful of Nuts

Non-fiction
Rain in the Mountains
Scenes from a Writer's Life
The Lamp Is Lit
The Little Book of Comfort
Landour Days
Notes from a Small Room

Anthologies
Classic Ruskin Bond: Complete and Unabridged
Classic Ruskin Bond Volume 2: The Memoirs
Dust on the Mountain: Collected Stories
The Best of Ruskin Bond
Friends in Small Places
Indian Ghost Stories (ed.)
Indian Railway Stories (ed.)
Classical Indian Love Stories and Lyrics (ed.)
Tales of the Open Road
Ruskin Bond's Book of Nature
Ruskin Bond's Book of Humour
A Town Called Dehra

Poetry
Ruskin Bond's Book of Verse

Maharani

RUSKIN BOND

PENGUIN BOOKS

PENGUIN BOOKS
Published by the Penguin Group
Penguin Books India Pvt. Ltd, 11 Community Centre, Panchsheel Park,
New Delhi 110 017, India
Penguin Group (USA) Inc., 375 Hudson Street, New York, New York 10014, USA
Penguin Group (Canada), 90 Eglinton Avenue East, Suite 700, Toronto,
Ontario, M4P 2Y3, Canada (a division of Pearson Penguin Canada Inc.)
Penguin Books Ltd, 80 Strand, London WC2R 0RL, England
Penguin Ireland, 25 St Stephen's Green, Dublin 2, Ireland (a division of
Penguin Books Ltd)
Penguin Group (Australia), 707 Collins Street, Melbourne, Victoria 3008,
Australia (a division of Pearson Australia Group Pty Ltd)
Penguin Group (NZ), 67 Apollo Drive, Rosedale, Auckland 0632,
New Zealand (a division of Pearson New Zealand Ltd)
Penguin Books (South Africa) (Pty) Ltd, Block D, Rosebank Office Park,
181 Jan Smuts Avenue, Parktown North, Johannesburg 2193, South Africa

Penguin Books Ltd, Registered Offices: 80 Strand, London WC2R 0RL, England

First published in Viking by Penguin Books India 2012
Published in Penguin Books 2013

Copyright © Ruskin Bond 2012

All rights reserved

10 9 8 7 6 5 4 3 2 1

ISBN 9780143420668

Typeset in Adobe Garamond Pro by Eleven Arts, New Delhi
Printed at Thomson Press India Ltd, New Delhi

ALWAYS LEARNING   **PEARSON**

Author's Note

Is this a true story?

Just because I am the narrator and play my part in it, this is not to be taken as autobiography or biography.

As in most of my work, characters are often based on people I have known or encountered over the years. But the events and situations in which they find themselves often bear little or no resemblance to actual events. In trying to write an engaging story, the author has often to juggle with people, places and happenings.

So this is not a true story. Nor is it a complete fabrication.

As Mark Twain said, 'Interesting if true. And if not true, still interesting.'

1

'I think I'm dying, Ruskin,' said H.H. as I took her hand and kissed it in the manner of some knight of old. She loved these little feudal courtesies.

'You must have said that a hundred times during the last ten years,' I said. 'You're dying for a drink, that's all. Shall I ask Seema to make some coffee? Then we can talk about these mortal coils that bind us.'

'You can't discuss life and death over a cup of coffee. Ask Seema to make a salad, and you go to the cabinet and fetch the bottle of vodka that dear old Sardar sahib from Faridkot brought me last week.'

H.H. (my old friend, the Maharani Sahiba of Mastipur) seldom bought any liquor, but her cabinet was full of bottles of wine, whisky, gin, sherry and various other liquids designed to make life more agreeable and interesting. These had been given to her by admirers, old and new, as well as those seeking funds or favours from her less-than-generous nature.

H.H. took her vodka neat, and I poured her a three-finger Patiala peg. I preferred mine with orange juice, but as I couldn't find any fruit juice in the cabinet, I took my Simla peg (two fingers) with soda and a slice of lemon. H.H. could drink me under the table, so I had to go carefully.

Soon we were in the throes of reminiscence.

H.H. (Neena to her close friends) always spoke in gloomy terms about the future, and spoke bitterly about her children and their deficiencies; but she grew quite animated when talking about the past, especially her own past and its more amorous episodes, of which there were many.

She had known me for years, ever since our school days, and as our relationship had never been a physical one, she found it easy to confide in me—knowing I would not make any overt demands—demands on her money (as from her many relations and dependants), or demands on her emotions (as from those who had been lovers). Sometimes she used me as a father confessor, but on this spring morning—April in the hills and the horse chestnut trees in blossom—she evinced one of those rare moments of concern for my own future and well-being.

'What on earth made you come back from England?' she asked. (It was a question she'd asked me many times.) 'You were young, you had a job, you had written a book—the future was all yours, if you wanted fame and money.'

'I followed my heart, not my head.'

'You were always thickheaded. What was it about India that brought you back all those years ago?'

'Romance,' I said.

'Romance!' She burst out laughing. 'There's nothing in the least romantic about you. You can't even *kiss* a girl properly.'

'It was the romance of India that brought me back.'

'Nothing romantic about this country. It's all politics, my dear.'

'Well, I've never bothered with the politics. Kept away from politicians and babudom as far as possible. But the romance that has been here for centuries, that's still here. The great plains, the desert, the forests, the seas breaking on our coasts, the mountains, the rivers, the down-to-earth people who belong to the land, the land itself . . . Do you know, I've never owned a square foot of land—not even enough for a grave—but I feel as though I own every square inch of land in this country. It's all mine, and no one can take it from me!' I wasn't usually so effusive, but Neena had got me going.

'The last romantic!'

'I suppose so.'

'Well, you were romantic enough when you wrote to me after that school social in Simla—how many years ago?'

'Hundreds.'

'Yes, it's better not to count. I was just fifteen then.'

'And I was a year older.'

H.H. was now well into her second Patiala peg, and I was just about to start on my second chotta Simla. A flood of memories overcame both of us.

'Do you remember that letter you wrote to me after the school social?'

'Of course I remember,' I said. 'It got me into trouble.'

Neena was in her final year at a residential school for girls. I was at an all-boys' boarding school—the 'Eton of the East' as someone once called it, although it had in fact been founded by a master from Rugby. We were the pride of Simla. All the 'royals' (the children of recently derecognized princely families) went to these schools. I was far from being 'royal'—my mother had some difficulty in paying my school fees—but I had done almost all my schooling in this most traditional of public schools, and as a senior prefect I felt I was on an equal footing with any prince or princess.

The senior boys had been invited to see a performance of *The Merchant of Venice* put on by the senior girls. To watch Shakespeare performed by amateurs is always a painful experience. We yawned and fidgeted through most of the play, but I was quite taken by the spirited performance of a bouncy, bright-eyed, rather squeaky-voiced girl who played Portia.

A week later we were invited to a 'social', a sort of dance party, at the girls' school, and the princess Neena very sportingly accepted my invitation to do the foxtrot. Sounds exciting, but the foxtrot was done at a crawl rather than a trot, and there was nothing foxy about it. Still, it gave you an opportunity to hold a girl in your arms while you shuffled slowly around the dance floor. A waltz would have been more invigorating, but the waltz required a certain amount of skill. Anyone, even the clumsiest of school boys, could foxtrot.

I was clumsy enough but I made up for this with what I thought was intelligent conversation. The princess did not say much, but she laughed easily, and she made no attempt to keep me at a distance. Soon her small breasts were pressed against me, her lips and cheeks within kissing range. Some enterprising soul turned off the lights, and in the darkness and confusion I gave her a quick peck on the cheek. I expected a slap in return, but instead I felt her salty lips (she'd been eating potato chips) pressed to mine. It was a sensation that sent a shiver down my spine (and elsewhere) and I wanted it to last forever. At sixteen, we want everything to last forever.

Back in school, I dashed off a sweetly worded love letter (those were the days of handwritten love notes)—I was good at them, and functioned as a letter-writer for other love-struck youths—and gave it to a day-scholar who had a sister in the girls' school. It was duly delivered, but no reply was forthcoming. I dashed off another, equally fervent, epistle; I even plagiarized a few lines from Jane Austen. No response. Perhaps I should have tried Shakespeare. *Love's Labour Lost* would have been appropriate.

Finally I sent a verbal message through the same courier service. There was an immediate response.

'What did she say?' I asked the messenger. 'What did she tell your sister?'

'She said you had pimples.'

∾

'Just the sort of thing you *would* say,' I remarked as we launched into another round of vodkas. Our conversation ran on like a river.

'But your letters were very nice, very romantic,' said H.H.

'I hope you didn't keep them.'

'You'd find them a bit embarrassing now, wouldn't

7

you? I *should* have kept them, just for a laugh. And to pass around at parties.'

'But you destroyed them, didn't you?' I asked anxiously.

'Yes, unfortunately. All that gushing nonsense.'

'A good thing love letters have gone out of fashion.'

'You weren't very good at kissing either. You slobbered all over me.'

'Well—never again.'

'Oh, but I like you when you're romantic. It reminds me of all those lovely films I saw when I was a girl. *Love Letters*, *Always in My Heart*, *Sweethearts*, *Bitter Sweet* . . . And those beautiful songs. I still sing them sometimes.'

She got up and moved unsteadily to the Steinway piano that took up one corner of the room. She sat down on the piano stool and banged out a few notes. 'Come on, sing with me, you romantic old fool!' And she began warbling the words of a Noël Coward song from *Bitter Sweet*:

I'll see you again,
Whenever spring breaks through again.

8

Time may lie heavy between,
But what has been
Is past forgetting . . .

Halfway through we broke down laughing. Seema appeared in the doorway, holding a tray on which lay a plate overflowing with sliced tomatoes.

H.H. shrieked with laughter.

'Where were you all this time, you silly girl? What took you so long?'

'There were no tomatoes, Rani-ma, so I went out to get some.'

'Clever girl. Can't have a salad without tomatoes.'

'But there's no lettuce. I couldn't find any lettuce.'

'Never mind, dear. Lettuce is really meant for rabbits. That's why they reproduce so quickly.'

And she broke into peals of laughter again.

'Come on, Ruskin, have some salad.'

'No, it's time for me to go. It's nearly four o'clock. But your guests—what do they have for lunch?'

'If they want lunch, they prepare it themselves. Take the salad away, dear. Give it to the monkeys. I'll go to bed for an hour or two.'

But before she could do so, there was a commotion

downstairs. Someone was standing at the gate and shouting up at the open window.

'It's Kartik,' said Seema anxiously. Kartik was H.H.'s elder son.

Neena rose from her chair and went to the window, hands on her hips.

'Send her down to me!' shouted the man at the gate. He looked dishevelled, his long hair uncombed, his face obscured by a week-long growth of beard. 'She's my woman, I'm going to marry her—you can't stop me!'

'He's drunk,' said H.H.

'That makes three of us,' I said.

I looked at Seema. She was trembling, biting her lip. 'Don't let him in, Rani-ma,' she pleaded.

'He can't come in, whether you're here or not,' snapped Neena. 'I'll get Hans to see him off!' She marched out of the room in search of Hans, her handyman, a Swiss acolyte she'd picked up at an ashram in the hills. Hans was a six-footer, with the build of a lumberjack. Kartik did not appear to be much more than five feet six inches. But he had a stentorian voice which carried clearly up to the window.

'Send that bitch down at once!' he yelled. 'She has all my money!'

I looked at Seema. She shook her head helplessly. 'He lost all his money in a card game.'

The gate had a lock on it, but Kartik was doing his best to climb over. He was almost over when big Hans, striding across the lawn like an angry stork, arrived at the gate and gave Kartik a shove, which sent him tumbling backwards on to the stony path. He got up with some difficulty. Then, cursing Hans, H.H. and Seema, he staggered away, vowing vengeance.

'You know him?' I asked the girl.

'We were engaged. But he beats me whenever he's drunk. He locked me up in a bathroom for a day and a night. I ran away when I had the chance. Rani-ma said I could stay with her. I have nowhere else to go. My home is near Ranchi. My parents are very poor. He met me there and promised me a good life. And so I came with him to Mussoorie.'

Before I left, I put my head in at the door of H.H.'s bedroom, intending to say goodbye. She was on her bed, flat on her back, snoring peacefully.

2

Neena was, of course, the second Maharani, the first having died in mysterious circumstances. I had never met the first, being a small boy at the time, but I remember my mother and her friend Doreen talking about her; speculating, rather, on the possible reasons for the young Maharani's early demise.

She was a pretty girl, the daughter of a raja from a small hill state. She had given her husband a male heir, so he could have had no complaints on that score. However, she was not the out-going, socializing type—disliked parties, abhorred the shikar expeditions so dear to His Highness, preferring to stay at home when he went off on a tiger hunt with his cronies. He wasn't much of a shot, and the mounted tiger heads on his palace walls were, in fact, his father's trophies. His Highness's gun had only accounted for the slow-footed sambar and a few wild boar caught unawares during their mid-afternoon siesta. Actually, His Highness's ambition was to capture and bring home a tiger cub so that one day he could boast of having a grown tiger padding about on his front lawn. This ambition stemmed from the fact that the Nawab of Dhol had a pet lioness which enjoyed the freedom of Dhol's palace grounds. If Dhol could keep a lion, why shouldn't Mastipur have a tiger? India and its millions won independence from Britain, and the privileged princes had been obliged to give up their kingdoms; but they still hung on to their titles, and many enjoyed great wealth. The words of a popular American song were no exaggeration:

Take my rubies and take my pearls,
Take my camels and take my girls,
I'm the rich Maharaja of Magador!

In point of fact, their generosity did not extend to bestowing their rubies and pearls on anyone they fancied. The smart ones hung on to the family jewels, or took them out of the country.

But to return to the Maharaja of Mastipur and his forays into the forests of the Doon. The Terai jungles were far more extensive then than they are now. So keen was His Highness on having a young tiger for a pet that he actually engaged the services of Jim Corbett, the celebrated big-game hunter, in his efforts to obtain one.

Corbett specialized in hunting man-eaters (or so he tells us in his books), but he was always ready to oblige royalty, and they would sometimes engage him to supervise VIP shikar parties—like the one for Lord Linlithgow, viceroy, in which a couple of tigers had to be rounded up and driven in the direction of the great man, who fired at them from the safety of his elephant's howdah. If he missed (and it often happened) Corbett would be conveniently placed to fire the fatal shot, attributing it to the guest of honour. He had, poor man, to make a living.

It was while the sport-loving Maharaja was away on his many forays into the forests of north India that his Maharani, bored with palace life and the novels of Baroness Orczy, whose Scarlet Pimpernel regularly saved the lives of French royalty during the Revolution, took to taking long drives around the surrounding countryside in her Hillman Minx (or sometimes Sunbeam-Talbot), the latest in fast cars.

The State employed three drivers, and the Maharani's favourite was Gafoor, a good-looking, good-natured Muslim youth who had been recommended by the Nawab of Dhol. Gafoor was the ideal employee—competent, courteous, willing to please, and exuding sex appeal.

From sitting in the back seat, the Maharani took to sitting in the front seat, beside the driver. It gave her a better view of the countryside, she said. (And a better view of Gafoor's handsome profile.) She left the palace seated at the back, but once they were out of town she transferred to the front of the car.

If a sex-starved Maharani has to spend several hours a day in the company of a virile young driver, she is bound to become attached to him.

Those drives into the countryside became more intimate. There were stops at small towns where the Maharani was anonymous. They dined together at dhabas and small cafés where royalty would never think of dining. And one evening, when the car broke down, they were forced to spend a night at a small hotel outside Saharanpur. They took separate rooms. But when, on retiring for the night, the Maharani complained of a headache, Gafoor was there with a small container of Oriental Balm which he applied gently to his employer's fevered brow.

It served only to make her more feverish. She sighed and moaned as his beautiful but rough fingers caressed her forehead, her temples, the lobes of her ears. His hands went to her breasts, his lips to her welcoming mouth. Five minutes of frantic kissing, and then they flung aside their garments, embraced, thrust at each other like gladiators lusting for love rather than blood.

Hers was a thirst that could not be quenched. The Maharaja had given her a son but little else. Years of loveless lovemaking had made her vulnerable to the first real lover who had come her way. Gafoor fitted the role perfectly. Well endowed, considerate, willing to give as much pleasure as he took, he was the ideal foil for this neglected but passionate princess. While His Highness hunted elusive tigers, his chauffeur tamed a real tigress in his master's very own den.

In Corbett, the Maharaja found the ideal companion. Neither was interested in sex. Corbett lived with his spinster sister. He was a man of the forests, well versed in jungle lore. Women were a distraction. He was a role model for the young Maharaja who aspired to a comparable reputation as big-game hunter.

But royalty is proud of its possessions, and his queen was one of his possessions. There were spies in the palace and it wasn't long before word reached him that there was more to the Maharani's outings with the driver than a desire for fresh air. Their intimacy had not gone unnoticed. It is hard for lovers to conceal their passion for each other. Little things gave them away—a glance, a gesture, a familiarity not usually found between mistress and servant.

The first to notice this increasing familiarity was a nun.

What was a nun doing in the Maharaja's palace? No one knew where she came from or where she went, but twice a year she turned up at the palace, stayed a few weeks and then disappeared again. The

Maharaja's mother had been part Hungarian, and the nun was a relative, or so it was assumed. A tall woman with full lips, hollowed-out eyes, and very big hands for a woman. The palace servants were convinced she was a man, or partly a man. One young scamp claimed to have peeped into her room from a skylight, when 'Sister' was removing her white habit, and had seen hairy legs and something peeping out from between them. 'You're just making it up,' said the cook, giving the boy a cuff over the ears. But speculation continued.

The good 'Sister' had noticed and observed the clandestine affair between Gafoor and Her Highness. So had everyone else, although they had chosen to ignore it. Why create trouble in a household that was otherwise running smoothly? But the nun was a confidante of the Maharaja. He would often turn to her for advice. Although far from being religious, he stood in awe of all those who had renounced the carnal pleasures of this world. A suggestion from Sister that he keep an eye on his queen's comings and goings—more frequent when he was away, chasing big cats—made him suspicious, deeply offended.

No king will tolerate a queen's infidelity, especially if her lover turns out to be one of his servants.

The Maharani and Gafoor had discovered a shady, fern-covered bank near a stream that came down from the hills. They would leave the car on a by-lane and walk down to the stream. The ferns provided a soft, inviting bed. Dragonflies hovered over their naked, thrusting bodies.

A magpie in a nearby tree gave an alarm call. Too late. The lovers were still entwined when a shadow fell across them. Someone held a 12-gauge shotgun to Gafoor's head and pulled the trigger. The young man's blood and brains splattered over the shrieking Maharani.

As the sound of the explosion died away, the queen's shrieks gave way to hysterical sobbing. She was dragged away. Gafoor's body was thrown into a nullah, to be feasted upon that night by jackals and other scavengers.

The birds kept up a racket for some time before silence returned to the forest.

∾

'And what happened to the Maharani?' asked Doreen, who felt a certain empathy with the tragic young queen, for she (Doreen) had been quite a beauty when young and had taken many young men as lovers.

'She died a few months later,' said my mother. 'Some say she died of a broken heart; others say she was poisoned. Slow poison, probably. The Maharaja had many doctors among his friends, and one of them provided the death certificate. All it said was heart failure.'

'But why slow poisoning? He could have had her shot at the same time that the driver was dispatched.'

'Maybe he wanted to prolong her misery, see her suffer. Some of those princes had sadistic natures. There was one who modelled himself on the emperor Nero. Created an arena where young men from his prisons were thrown into a ring of tigers. He loved watching them being torn apart.'

'So he wanted to watch his young queen dying. And taunted her too, I expect,' said Doreen. 'He must have known something about poisons.'

'He left that to the nun,' said my mother. 'Sister Clarissa. Apparently she'd been a trained nurse before she went into a nunnery.'

'And how did she get out of the nunnery?'

'God knows. I suppose they get leave from time to time.'

'Sounds fishy to me,' said Doreen. 'I doubt if she was really a nun. And when the Maharani died, how did he take it?'

'Started looking for another,' said my mother. 'Only this time, he wanted someone who could shoot tigers.'

Which was where Neena came in.

Neena the jungle princess, Neena of the nine lives.

She was only sixteen, just out of school, when she was married to His Highness, some twenty years her senior; but she was a willing partner on his shikar trips, and even cosied up to Jim Corbett when the great man wasn't tracking man-eating tigers. But Corbett seemed immune to the lures of beautiful women.

'Couldn't get it up,' she told me, years later. 'He lived with his sister, no sex life at all. I think he was impotent. Instead of having sex, he shot tigers. Once, in camp, my hand brushed against his trousers—quite inadvertently, of course—but there was nothing there! He pushed my hand away and gave me his gun to hold instead!'

'Lucky you,' I remember saying. 'His fans would have given anything to hold his gun.'

'Well, there was nothing else to hold. And yet, there was a story going around that he was in love with me.'

'Platonic, no doubt. Everyone was in love with you.'

3

A week or two later, in the first week of May, I paid another visit to H.H. at her Mussoorie home. The walk from my cottage to the 'palace'—a distance of three miles—was rather more arduous than it used to be. Our schooldays were long behind us and age had caught up.

She was sitting in the sun, under a garden umbrella, a gin and tonic on the table beside her.

'I think I'll die this year, Ruskin,' she said. This was her usual mid-morning greeting.

'You're Neena of the nine lives,' I said.

'I've used them all up. There aren't any left. Sit down and have a gin.'

Seema had seen me arrive and, assuming that I was going to join Neena in some gin and gossip, came over with a glass and a decanter of water. A bottle of Gilbey's dry gin was already conveniently placed near Neena's easy chair. H.H. poured me a stiff one.

'I'm not really a heavy drinker,' she said. 'I drink till late afternoon, then I have an early supper and go to bed.'

'Were you drinking when you were married? Did you drink with His Highness?'

'Never. He did enough drinking for the two of us—or more. Without a drink he was like a fish out of water. Kartik takes after him. Karan has other vices.' She was referring to her sons, both middle-aged layabouts, surviving on the modest allowance she allowed them. Kartik was now a hopeless alcoholic. Karan was still experimenting with various drugs. I did not want to talk about them.

'His Highness, your husband—had he no other interests apart from hunting and drinking?'

'Hobbies, you mean? Well, he kept white rats. You knew about that, I suppose.'

'No, never heard of them. White rats! As pets? When I was a boy, there were one or two boys who kept them.'

'Well, my husband was always a boy. He never did grow up. His favourite reading was Billy Bunter.'

'The Fat Boy of the Remove. Forever eating. I read Billy Bunter too.'

'Yes, but you went on to Virginia Woolf. Or didn't you?'

'I did, but I can still enjoy Bunter. And William. All the bad boys. And speaking of Bunter, I'm hungry. Is your diet entirely liquid?'

As though on cue, Seema appeared with a dish of pakoras. She was now Neena's slave. She gave me a radiant smile. I basked in its glow. When a seventy-year-old receives a ravishing smile from a twenty-year-old, the years simply fall away. On a spring morning too. A couple of bulbuls had been twittering away, without getting my attention. Now they began to sound like tender songsters. Ah, the sweet mystery of life!

Neena brought me back to earth.

'Stop looking at her, and look at me for a change,' she snapped. 'You're far too old and useless to be ogling pretty tribal girls.'

'No harm in ogling,' I said. 'But we were on the subject of Virginia Woolf.'

'White rats.'

'Your husband's hobby. How many did he have—five or six?'

'Five or six? Hundreds! There were hundreds of them. Well, he started with three or four. But rats are oversexed little devils, forever fornicating. They multiply like—like rats! Within a couple of years there were over a hundred rats. All over the place!'

'All over the palace?'

'They had a wing of this mansion to themselves,' said Neena pointing to a large empty space between one wing of the building and the servants' quarters. 'I had it pulled down after my husband died. I suppose it could have been of use, but it stank to high heaven—the boards were well pickled in rat urine.'

'What happened to the rats? You let them all loose, I suppose.'

'Had to hunt them down. They didn't want to leave the grounds. Not after the last grand meal they'd enjoyed. Don't you know about it? I thought everyone knew, although we did try to hush it up. It did not seem appropriate, somehow, for a maharaja of the realm to be consumed by his pets. Yes, the rats made a meal of him. I wasn't here, thank god; I was overseeing repairs to our palace in Mastipur—it was in a dreadful condition. And His Highness, being on his own without anyone to control his excesses, went on a binge, drank his way through all the whisky and brandy in the house—and then decided he would say goodnight to his pets, see that they had been fed and given water and lots of cotton-wool to nest in. There was a boy who did the chores, but it was his day off, and His Highness decided he'd look in on them, make sure they were comfortable. He'd installed a toy train for them, and sometimes he'd give them train rides around the room, placing his favourites in open carriages, winding up the engine, and watching it carry a trainful of squeaking rats going around in circles while he sat on a stool, watching them and chuckling with delight.

'Well, that night he'd had too much to drink—far too much—and he fell off his stool and passed out. Completely blotto—and there was no one around to pick him up and carry him to his bedroom. It was well past midnight. The rats were hungry. Hundreds of hungry, angry rats! Soon they were all over him, exploring his clothes, wriggling into his underwear, nibbling here and there. Nibble, nibble, snap! Word soon got around. Their affectionate master was tasty. And he didn't seem to mind being nibbled and bitten and chewed. Had he been conscious he would have struggled, cried out, attempted to crawl out of the room. But he was completely anaesthetized—paralysed—mercifully unaware of what was happening to him.

'The rats were delighted. This was better than biscuits and bread. Sweet, juicy steaks! A delicious rump! A belly to feast on and thighs dripping blood. No part of his anatomy went to waste. Even his eyes were gouged out. They gnawed at his heart, burrowed into his brain. By morning the rats were satiated, most of them asleep, a few still looking for pickings.

'When the boy came in, he found a skeleton and a bundle of clothes. At first he did not know whose bones lay scattered about the room—then he recognized His Highness's embroidered slippers and he went screaming from the room and woke up the rest of the household.

'I arrived next day, and a funeral was arranged.

We cremated what was left of him down in Rajpur. Dr Gupta was very helpful, as always. I gave him a bottle of Scotch and he made out the death certificate. Heart failure, of course, what else? And it was perfectly true. His heart must have stopped long before the rats got to it.

'So now you know the true story, my dear. Aren't you going to stay for lunch? Hans is making mutton cutlets today. But you're not hungry. Well, have another gin, and then we'll go inside and I'll give you something.'

It was seldom that Neena gave anything away, and I was intrigued by her offer. And after hearing her account of the Maharaja's gruesome end, I needed another drink. But I excused myself from lunch, promising to feast on Hans's mutton cutlets another time.

Before I left, Neena led me into a small dressing room which was attached to her bedroom.

'This is what I wanted to give you,' she said, giving me an affectionate peck on the cheeks. 'I think it will fit. You're about His Highness's size.'

She opened a cupboard to reveal an elegant sherwani draped over a coat hanger.

'You've looked after it so carefully,' I said. 'Why do you want to give it away?'

'Because you're such a dear friend. I wouldn't give it to anyone. That ragged old overcoat you wear every winter makes you look like a tramp.'

'It's too grand for me,' I said, turning away and still thinking of rats. 'Keep it for someone special.'

4

Men friends?

She'd had a few. A professor, a surgeon, a brigadier . . . But the most charming of them all had been the diplomat from Bolivia (or was it Chile? or Peru?). And since he's still around somewhere (and probably carrying a gun) we'll just call him Ricardo. One can always fall back on Hollywood for a colourful, swashbuckling name.

After leaving school I saw nothing of Neena for a number of years—just heard about her from time to time—and when I did meet her, just briefly, she was

31

the mother of two spoilt little brats and the owner of a posh little seafront hotel in Pondicherry.

I had been commissioned by a travel magazine to write an article on three former French enclaves in India—Chandernagore, Mahé, Pondicherry—and that was my reason for being on the Beach Road in Pondicherry on a breezy, late monsoon evening, wending my way through a colourful and fairly conservative crowd of locals and Tamilian holiday-makers. The sea was calm, the seagulls preoccupied, the seafront given over to children with ice cream cones, when a commotion at one end of the esplanade caught my attention.

Promenaders scattered as a goat came charging through them, followed by a yapping Pekinese on a leash. The owner of the dog and the leash was nowhere in sight. A goat in full flight, followed by a furious peke, is a sight to behold. A Pekinese gone berserk will take on a tiger, and no one was going near it. Having grown up among my mother's dogs, yapping Poms and snapping dachshunds, I had some idea of how to handle them; and grabbing the leash, I managed to halt the advance of the canine terrorist—so suddenly that it sprang into the air and almost throttled itself. I picked it up, holding it at arm's length to prevent it from biting my nose off, and looked around for its owner. A few spectators were clapping. I was a hero at last.

But not for long. A young woman in a billowing skirt advanced on me, accompanied by a large, unfriendly looking boxer. I had not grown up with these larger breeds. Fortunately it was on a leash, and the leash was in the hands of its owner, who looked slightly familiar.

'You can put it down now,' she said, indicating the wriggling peke. 'And give me the leash. Betsy is a good little dog, but she doesn't like goats. They get into our compound and eat all the petunias.'

'Betsy,' I said. 'Like Aunt Betsy Trotwood. She didn't like donkeys. They kept getting into her garden.'

'You had an aunt called Betsy?'

'No. Betsy Trotwood in *David Copperfield*.'

'Is that a film?'

'No, ma'am, it's a book. But you're right, it was a film too.'

'I don't read many books. Only bestsellers. Like *Forever Amber*. Have you read *Forever Amber*?'

'No, ma'am.'

'She was a whore.'

'Wonderful.'

She looked hard at me, then said, 'I think I've seen you before.'

'I think I've seen you too,' I said. 'Can't forget a pretty face.'

'You're that boy who danced with me at the school social!' she exclaimed, dropping both leashes and giving me a great hug and a kiss. 'My dream lover!'

We were attracting a certain amount of attention and I was feeling terribly embarrassed. Unlike Goa, the Pondicherry beach is on the conservative side.

'You're blushing,' she observed.

'You're Neena,' I said. 'Weren't you a princess?'

'I'm still a princess. Better still, I'm a queen— married to H.H. the Maharaja of Mastipur. Not that he's anything to boast about. But come back with me and have a coffee. Here, you hold Betsy and I'll hold the boxer. You're a dog lover, aren't you?'

'Actually, I prefer goldfish. They don't bark. Or bite.'

'Silly,' she said, and taking me by the hand, led me across the Beach Road and up the steps of a gaily painted seafront hotel. The dogs were let loose and settled down in the veranda. It was hot outside. I was dripping like an ice cream cone.

'This hotel is yours?' I asked.

'A present from my dear husband. So that I don't get too bored in his absence. Actually, I rather enjoy running it. One meets interesting people—like you, for instance.'

'I'm staying somewhere more modest. Can't afford this place.'

'You can be my guest, dear. Old school pals and all that.'

'How long ago was it? You were very pretty.'

'I don't like your use of the past tense.'

'Forgive me. You've gone from being pretty to being ravishingly beautiful. Like Elizabeth Taylor. She was pretty in *National Velvet*, beautiful in *Raintree County*, and when she played a real queen, in *Cleopatra*, she was a bit—' I hesitated, searching for the right word.

'Ravishing?'

'No, a bit dowdy, actually.'

For this observation I received a clip across the ear. She pushed me into an easy chair, or rather sofa, and plonked herself down beside me.

'So, are you calling me dowdy?'

'No, I'm comparing you to Elizabeth Taylor. One of the world's most beautiful women. And a fine actress.'

She joined me on the sofa. 'I wasn't such a bad actress, was I?'

'No, in that school play, *The Merchant of Venice*, you caught everyone's attention. And I bet you can still act.'

'I'm acting all the time. Acting for my husband, acting for my children, acting for the servants. It's only with someone like you that I can feel a bit free.'

'Down to earth. That's your true nature.'

She was silent for some time. I could hear voices outside, and the occasional plaint of a seagull, but the veranda was bathed in silence.

'Most of the world's troubles are created by impotent men,' she said, quite unexpectedly. 'Hitler, Napoleon, Julius Caesar—none of them were any good in bed—so they made up for it by imposing their will on the rest of mankind—making sure that everyone was under their thumbs since they couldn't be under their dicks! Do I shock you?'

'Not at all. You represent a good convent education. I presume you include your husband, the Maharaja, among the impotent elite.'

'Shut up. And come closer. You're not afraid of me, are you?'

'Your manager is staring at us from the lobby. And your dog has a firm grip on my ankle.'

'Yes, he's very protective.'

'The manager or the peke?'

'Both. And he's not my manager. He's the father of the boy who saved me from drowning.'

'He must have been a brave boy and a good swimmer. I'd like to meet him.'

'You can't. He drowned.'

Neena was always full of surprises. Her every action seemed to set off a chain of actions and reactions that affected others more than it did her.

'What happened?'

'I swam too far out.'

I looked out across the Beach Road. People were strolling about, but no one was bathing.

'Do people swim here?'

'Of course not, stupid. Early morning it's just a public toilet. You have to go out to Serenity Beach if you want to swim.'

'And you're a good swimmer.'

'Well, I used to be. Before I gave birth to a couple of monsters. Anyway, I swam too far, tired myself out, started drifting with the current. I went under a couple of times. I was quite helpless. Then this boy came along. He was from one of the fishing boats. He held me up until one of the boats came along and the men fished me out of the water. But they couldn't get to him. A strong current swept him away. I didn't see him drown, thank god. They told me afterwards.'

'You were very lucky. You're a cat with nine lives.'

'Are you calling me a cat?'

'Well, bitches aren't so lucky. Cats can get away with almost anything.'

'I suppose that's true. Do you know, when I was a toddler I almost drowned in a bucket of water.'

'That must have been difficult.'

'Not at all. Someone had left a bucket of water on the veranda steps and I tumbled into it, head first. I was just two at the time. One of my cousins, a little older than me, saw me in the bucket with feet waving in the air. He pulled me out.'

'He deserved a medal.'

'He got a beating from our parents. They thought he'd pushed me in.'

'Didn't you tell them how it happened?'

'How could I? I was only two. All I could do was point at him and cry, "Vijay, Vijay!" That was his name.'

'Poor Vijay. For the rest of his life he would be unwilling to help a damsel in distress. What became of him?'

'He became a vet.'

'Ah! Saving animals was obviously more rewarding than saving little princesses.'

∿

Neena invited me to accompany her to a spiritual discourse at the Aurobindo Ashram. She was already showing an interest in 'spirituality' as a sort of balance to the more physical side of her nature. Over the years she was to flirt with religion, spirituality, even the philosophy of such mental disciplinarians as the Theosophists and Gurdjieff; but always her

physicality, her sensuous nature, her enjoyment of
the good things of life, overcame her brief periods
of renunciation and austerity.

I had never suffered from a conflict of bodily and
spiritual interests—being quite happy to go along
with the physical and mental make-up that had come
to me with my genes—and I had no hesitation in
declining the invitation to self-improvement.

As I descended the steps of the hotel, I passed
two youngsters accompanied by their nanny. They
weren't more than five years old, with just over a
year's difference in their ages. The younger one was
quite cocky, making faces at passers-by, including
me. The other had an abnormally large head, with
large, protruding eyes. I recalled that Neena had
married her first cousin, which may have accounted
for the abnormalities. Marriages amongst cousins
were not uncommon in princely families. After all,
there were only a certain number of kingdoms in the
land. If you wanted to forge a link with another State
through your son or daughter, there was always the
chance that they would be marrying a relative.

The nanny was unusual—not an ayah or a
conventional nanny, but a nun, tall and stately, attired

in a spotless white habit. I couldn't see much of her face, but I got the impression that she was middle-aged, fair complexioned. She swept past without a look in my direction. Long strides like a man's. I remembered the story of the nun who had nursed the first Maharani, right up to the end. Could she have been the same person?

5

After some time, even the strongest of ties begin to fray. That's one of the sad things about life—our human inability to sustain our love for each other with the same abiding intensity. Time takes its toll. We remember each other with affection but we are no longer prepared to dash across continents to hold the hand of friend or former lover—unless it happens to be one's own offspring. And even then . . .

In any case, Neena and I were never lovers or inseparable friends. Just two people who had been attracted to each other, who found each other interesting, thought the world a funny place to live in, had some things in common, kept in touch in a haphazard way, but did not miss each other very much. What Neena wanted out of life was something very different from what I wanted out of life.

And what did I want of life? I had promised myself much, but achieved little. A few years in Delhi had all but extinguished my creative spark. All I could write about were old tombs and monuments, and after some time I felt as dead as those who had been interred in these handsome cenotaphs. Living in the new capital, I felt like an outsider—often I was made to feel like one—for I had not been through the upheaval experienced by the refugees from western Punjab. Model Town, Rajouri Garden, Patel Nagar's east, south and west were their citadels, and I lived there on sufferance. I felt at home only in Old Delhi, in the Civil Lines, Kashmere Gate, and the leafy lanes of Lutyens' New Delhi where, as a small boy, I had lived with my father in barracks or in rented rooms on Atul Grove Lane. I had given up on Dehra Dun, my 'hometown', but I felt drawn to the hills, where living seemed a little more meaningful and resonant.

To wake at dawn and watch the rosy glow of approaching daybreak before the sun stroked its way over the mountains was, for me, a never-ending delight. And still is, forty years later.

∽

That move to the hills did lead to a rejuvenation, at least as far as my writing went. In the cottage I rented there was a window seat looking out upon a sociable gathering of trees: maple, oak, rhododendron, long-leaved pine—providing a recreation ground for long-tailed blue magpies, bulbuls, minivets and the occasional paradise flycatcher—and here I spent the mornings, turning out stories, poems, essays, children's tales, anything that came to mind, some of these compositions bringing in a few cheques from time to time. And here, my interest in dendrology came to fruition.

I was entirely on my own, eating out of tins or experimenting with omelettes—some day I must write my bestselling cookery book, *100 Failed Omelettes*—and occasionally taking a meal at a dhaba near the bus stand. I went for long walks—I did a lot of walking in those days—and some of these walks took me up to the heights of Landour or down to the vale of Barlowganj or out to Happy Valley, where the Tibetan refugees had been resettled.

Barlowganj, once the property of a long-forgotten General Barlow, now a straggling bazaar on the old Kipling Road, leading down past several large estates and princely villas, was empty for most of the year. Summer homes for the rich and famous.

Some of the buildings had survived for over a century, and some of the names too. 'Seven Oaks' (the original owner must have come from Kent), 'Arundel' (shades of Sir Walter Scott), 'Wynberg' (a South African connection), and 'Bala Hissar' (an Afghan connection).

The old Bala Hissar estate is now a school, and not many know that it was once the residence-in-exile of an Afghan king, deposed and replaced by the British after the Afghan wars of the 1840s. But I was more interested in a house some way below its ramparts, a quaint rambling building that went by the name of 'Hollow Oak'. Didn't an English king hide from his pursuers in the hollow of a giant oak until he was discovered and beheaded? I peered over the iron gate trying to see if there were any giant or hollow oaks on the premises. There were none. Perhaps they had been done away with to make room for more buildings. But trailing over the old stone wall was a branch of wisteria, its heady perfume pervading the vicinity.

In the garden two children were playing—a slim boy who must have been thirteen or fourteen and a girl of ten or eleven. The girl was on a swing, singing to herself. The boy sat on a stone bench, looking bored. While the girl looked pretty and vivacious, the boy had a sullen, brooding beauty, accentuated by the shifting shadows of maple leaves which played about his face. The oaks were in new leaf, their tender milky green catching the soft late afternoon sunlight, while the Japanese maples were sending out leaf buds in flame orange turning to red and then dark green as they unfolded. The boy looked up at me, his eyes in the sunlight an unusual shade of green, sheltered by long, dark lashes. He had been cutting pictures out of a magazine. Intent on this work, he gave me no more than a glance. The girl saw me but took no notice. She was used to seeing strangers at the gate.

From the house came sounds of music and

merriment. Someone was singing, tunelessly, in an effort to outdo the pop group whose latest record was being played at full volume, its sentiments somehow diminished by the surrounding mountains.

A window opened, a hand beckoned. Was I being invited to join the party?

I was in no mood to join an afternoon dance party, and I was still a stranger in those parts, unsure of my neighbours, so I returned the wave with a friendly wave of my own, and continued on my walk.

෴

That evening, growing restless, I went to the cinema. In those days, before television entered every home, people went to the pictures, and the hill station boasted of at least five cinema halls, albeit small theatres.

The Picture Palace was showing a slapstick comedy, an amalgam of silent shorts featuring Buster Keaton, Harry Langdon, the Keystone Kops, and my old friends Laurel and Hardy. I loved these comic geniuses of another era, and though I was a little late for the evening show, I slipped in and took a seat about midway down the hall. Already a bit short-sighted, I avoided the more expensive seats at the back. The seats up front were in poor shape, very uncomfortable, and often infested with fleas, but at least they gave me a clear view of the action on screen.

As much as I was enjoying the picture, the customer on the seat just in front of me was enjoying it even more. He giggled, laughed out loud, squirmed in his seat, even jumped up and down with delight whenever the custard pies started flying, as they did with increasing frequency. Those custard-pie fights were always great to watch—the timing was perfect, complete anarchy transformed into ballet, as everyone on the set entered into the spirit of the thing, flinging pies in all directions. In today's movies, cars pile up in crazy contortions—not always funny—and I suppose cars are expendable in the way custard pies were expendable in the silent era. Cars colliding with each other make a horrible sound. Twisted metal and broken bones. Throwing a custard pie was an art in itself. The tradition should be revived.

When the lights came on I found that my fellow connoisseur of silent comedy was just a boy—the same boy I had seen in the Barlowganj garden earlier that day.

He passed me on his way out, and gave me a conspiratorial smile—as though to say, 'You shared in my happiness. I heard your laughter too.'

6

In the sixties and early seventies they were still using hand-pulled rickshaws in the hill station. These rickshaws could seat two adults and one or two small children. Two men pulled, two pushed. The Maharajas and their consorts—and there were several who made Mussoorie their playground or pleasure resort—had their own well-maintained rickshaws, drawn by liveried footmen, and it was one of these that stopped outside my creaking wooden gate early that summer.

The footmen wore turbans and uniforms but were

barefooted. These poor, uneducated hillmen from the interior came to the hill station to earn a living and often ended up as rickshaw-pullers. The healthier village boys went into the army; the discards pulled rickshaws. Little grew on the rocky mountain soil, and they and their families had to eat. The soles of their feet were hard and calloused. They were strong in the arms and legs, but their lungs were weak and many of them suffered from tuberculosis, dying before they were thirty.

The young man who alighted from this rickshaw was an apparition in clashing colours—pink T-shirt, green trackpants, embroidered Ladakhi boots. He had rings on all his fingers—they glowed with emeralds, rubies and sapphires; even a thumb was encased in a gold ring. He looked like a caricature of an old-time prince, except that he was a real prince and most anxious to let you know it.

'I'm Prince Kartik of Mastipur,' he announced. 'My mother sent me to see you. She wants you to come to dinner. Tomorrow night. Quite informal, of course.'

'Do I know your mother?'

'You're Mr Bond, aren't you?'

'That's right, Ruskin.'

'Funny name.'

'Well, have a good laugh. They say it's good for the heart.'

He frowned, unsure as to whether or not he should feel offended. Obviously a sense of humour was not one of his attributes.

'I'll try to come,' I said. 'But where's the palace?'

'It's called Hollow Oak. Not far from here.'

'I think I know it. I passed by the other day. There was a party going on.'

'We have lots of parties. My mother gives great parties.'

For Neena, H.H., life was one long party—or so it seemed.

Her bejewelled brat of a son got on to his rickshaw and waved his flunkeys on. The only thing that was missing was a whip.

I wasn't feeling very sociable at the time—I had come to the hills to write, to wander, to be far from the city—and I wasn't sure that I wanted to see Neena again. But I went anyway.

∽

Well, she still kept pekes—the breed I disliked most—as I discovered when I opened the gate of Hollow Oak and walked up the driveway, only to be set upon by three yapping, snapping, bug-eyed members of this unappealing species of canine ill breeding. One snapped at my ankles; one tore at my trousers; the third appeared to be having a cataleptic fit as it endeavoured to get between my legs and trip me up.

I was rescued by a couple of urchins, the chowkidar's grandchildren, as it turned out—who drove them off and led me to the front door.

The party was in full swing and I entered with some trepidation.

Rock music was bouncing off the walls, and several unidentifiable persons of indeterminate ages were gyrating around the room, totally oblivious to my presence.

'Hello!' I called, stepping into the room. 'Good evening!'

No one paid me the slightest attention.

I was on the point of turning around and leaving when a large-bosomed, broad-bottomed lady in red grabbed hold of me, gathered me in her arms, and swept me across the floor to the far end of the long room. She then took off with another partner.

And then I found Neena. She had a glass of whisky in one hand, and a half empty bottle of whisky balanced on her head.

She was pacing up and down in front of a makeshift bar, the bottle on her head.

When she saw me she gave a cry of recognition. She sprang forward and the bottle fell to the floor, where it lay shattered, leaking precious fluid.

'Now look what you've done,' she said, blaming me for the disaster but giving me a kiss all the same. Then she burst into song:

Ten green bottles standing on a wall,
If one green bottle should accidentally fall,
There'll be nine green bottles standing on the wall.

Everyone joined in, and the song continued on its merry way while a barefoot servant padded in and cleaned up the mess.

'You're looking cute,' said Neena, giving me another peck on the cheek.

'And you're looking younger than ever,' I lied,

since it seemed to be a time for hollow compliments. She looked pleased.

'Flattery will get you everywhere,' she said. 'Come, dance with me.'

I was never much of a dancer, but as Neena was far from steady on her feet, my own clumsiness went unnoticed. We staggered across the room, bumped into a drinks trolley, and knocked over a stuffed leopard.

Extricating myself from the moth-eaten trophy, I said, 'This must have been one of His Highness's conquests.'

'No, I was the one who shot it. My husband was given the first shot, but he missed. He missed out on most things. But that's another story. You must meet my new friends. They're very special.'

A tall, good-looking man of about forty was smiling at me, hand extended.

'This is Ricardo,' she said, putting a hand on his arm in a gesture of ownership. 'He's from Bolivia.'

'Cultural attaché in the Bolivian Embassy,' he added by way of further enlightenment.

I shook his hand and told him I was a writer.

'And what do you write?' he asked politely.

'Romantic drivel,' said Neena, butting in.

'I didn't know you were one of my fans,' I said.

'Well, you must meet my wife,' said the diplomat diplomatically. 'She reads romantic novels.'

I was introduced to the wife. Mrs Montalban. Not half as glamorous as the diplomat. Rather plain, in fact. She wore glasses; little or no make-up; a dress more suitable for office than a party. Almost as though she wanted to go unnoticed. By contrast, her husband was flashy, glamorous, the Latin extrovert, the Valentino type. But she was trim, in good shape.

She said she would love to read my books. I told her there were only two, and one of them was for children.

'My daughter reads a lot,' she said. I followed her gaze to the top of the stairwell, where two children sat crouching, watching the proceedings—the same children I had seen before in the garden.

'Pablo can come down if he wants to, but he's shy.'

'Pablo?'

'We named him after Picasso, but it's Anna who paints.'

'And what does Pablo do?'

'Dreams.'

Neena grabbed me by the arm and led me away to meet her other guests. A magistrate who wrote poetry. A dental surgeon. A faded princess. An overweight aunt (the lady in red). And Prince Kartik and his friends, a noisy bunch, who were having a party of their own at one end of the hall. The young prince was drunk. He gave me a welcoming hiccup and subsided into an armchair. His friends paid no attention to me or to Neena, but carried on dancing.

'Where's your younger son?' I asked.

'He's at boarding school. Expelled last year, but they had to take him back. The chairman of the board is an old friend.'

'What did he do?'

'Made love to me, of course.'

'Not the chairman. Your son.'

'Oh, he was caught smoking pot. They all do, you know, this younger generation. Ever since the Beatles came to Rishikesh.'

'Well, if he can sing like a Beatle, we'll forgive him.'

Prince Kartik's friends were doing their best to sing like the Beatles, but with only limited success. Anyone passing the house that night might easily have mistaken their efforts for the baying of wolves or jackals.

We retreated to the bar at the far end of the room. I observed that it was well stocked with the choicest of wines, brandy, cognac and Scotch whisky.

'All thanks to Ricardo,' said Neena. 'Whatever I want, he'll turn up with it.'

'Is he staying some time?'

'Only a week. Then we're off to Nepal.'

'His family too?'

'No, just Ricardo and me. The family will be here. The children will be going to that school next door.'

Ricardo passed us at that moment. Playing the host as though he'd always been master of the house, he was escorting a guest to the door. The doctor was leaving early. I watched Neena as she watched Ricardo. She had the aspect of a caged tiger watching its keeper approach with the day's hunk of juicy red meat. She was ready to pounce on her meat. And she wasn't going to share it with anyone.

An ornate wall clock struck midnight, but the drinking and dancing continued. There was no sign of any dinner. Neena could sustain herself on a purely liquid diet, and so could most of her guests. But I was growing hungry. I looked around for snacks but even the peanut bowls were empty.

Mrs Montalban was beckoning me from the next room. She put a plate of cutlets in my hands.

'I can see you're hungry,' she said. 'You'd better have some of the children's dinner.'

'Where are they?'

'They've eaten and gone to bed. Plenty of mutton cutlets left. You eat mutton?'

'Everything,' I said. 'Desperate writers can't be fussy.'

'Nor can desperate housewives,' she said, and helped herself to a cutlet. She seemed a homely sort of person, and I warmed to her.

'I think I'll slip away,' I said, 'but I hope to see you again.'

'We are here.'

I wished her goodnight and left the house by the kitchen door, walking around the building and through the garden—or what had once been a formal, ornamental garden. It had been neglected for some time. Bright moonlight shone on untrimmed rose bushes and paths that were a tangle of ivy and irises gone wild.

As I opened the gate, I was startled by an apparition. A tall figure in white came floating towards me.

It stopped and turned to look at me. I made out a long, sallow face of indeterminate age, the eyes deep-set, malevolent, and recognized the ghostly figure. It was the household's pet nun, the same white-robed Sister who had been nanny to Neena's two brats.

Was she a real nun, I wondered, and if so, why wasn't she in a convent or a nunnery instead of wandering about the Hollow Oak grounds. Or was she just a sinister figure in fancy dress?

Either way, she sent a shiver down my spine.

I did not stop to talk to her, but made a quick exit from the grounds.

The strident dance music followed me for some way before being dissipated by the enveloping silence of the mountains.

A pair of foxes were dancing a jig in the bright moonlight. A nightjar called, tonk-tonk. A street dog sang to the moon.

Everyone was having a party.

7

In those years, Neena was something of a hedonist. Widowed early, she had made the pursuit of pleasure her principal object in life. I think she wanted to cram all the fun that was possible into the few years of comparative youth that remained to her. And she didn't care if others were hurt in the process.

Ricardo was a catch that she had no intention of relinquishing—not for some time anyway.

She told Mrs Montalban to look upon the palace as her own home, albeit with her husband in absentia, and then took off with the obliging diplomat on a grand tour of beach resorts—Goa, the Maldives, Pondicherry where she still owned the hotel—and Nepal.

Mrs Montalban and the children had everything they wanted, but they were ill at ease in Hollow Oak. The nun appeared to be in charge, looking after the expenses and ordering the servants about. Prince Kartik showed up from time to time, complaining that he hadn't received his monthly allowance, 'Mummy' being preoccupied with other matters. The younger prince phoned from his school, demanding pocket money, and the nun would send him a money order.

And how were the Montalban children getting on? Anna was busy painting landscapes. Pablo, hands in pockets, whistling cheerfully, was loafing about on the Mall, drifting in and out of the cinema halls.

We met again at the Rialto. The film was *Gunfight at the O.K. Corral*. It turned out we were both fans of action-filled westerns. He sat next to me and we exchanged notes on our favourite western heroes. He liked Clint Eastwood, who had recently arrived on the screen with the 'spaghetti' western. I mentioned

Gary Cooper, but he was too young to have heard of him. This was before the coming of the video, so there was no way of catching up with the classics.

While the film was on, Pablo took no notice of me, even though he had seen me sitting a couple of seats away. He was totally absorbed in the on-screen action, even clapping his hands when the big gunfight climaxed to his satisfaction. There was something very innocent, even old-fashioned, about his enthusiasm. It reminded me of a performance of *Peter Pan*, which I had seen at a London theatre in the 1950s. When Tinker Bell was dying the audience was told she could be saved only if the audience declared that they believed in fairies. We were asked to clap our hands if we believed in fairies. Everyone clapped—or almost everyone—and Tinker Bell was saved. Not that the audience really believed in fairies. But they went along with the spirit of the play and the spirit of the playwright, that master of whimsy, J.M. Barrie.

Outside the hall, Pablo came up to me and asked, 'Did you like the movie?'

'Loved it,' I said to please him.

'The gunfight was great, wasn't it?'

'Super.'

'Did you like Wyatt Earp or Doc Holliday?'

'Both.'

'Doc Holliday drank too much. Like my father. And the Maharani.'

'She can drink more than Doc Holliday. And she's a better shot with a rifle.'

He smiled, gazed at me in a conspiratorial way. He had beautiful green eyes. His complexion was olive. He had full, sensual lips. There was something feminine about him, his hair long and black and glossy, his long hands full of gestures, his voice musical, as yet unbroken.

'Do you think they would give me a poster?' he asked unexpectedly.

I was amused. And sympathetic. I remembered my lonely boyhood, expeditions to various cinemas, sometimes in out-of-the-way places (Chandni Chowk, Meerut, even the suburbs of London), and the care and enthusiasm with which I would collect publicity leaflets, film magazines, postcards of favourite stars.

Mr Ahuja, the manager of the Rialto, was sitting in his office. I went up to him and asked, 'Do you have a spare poster that you can give this boy? He's a regular customer.'

He looked up and smiled. 'We've used them all up for this picture. But here are the posters for our next attraction. It will run for a week. *My Fair Lady*. Do you like musicals?'

'He likes posters.'

The manager laughed. 'Well, I can spare one, I think. Since you're regulars.' He rolled up a fairly large wall poster and handed it to me. I handed it to Pablo. He was thrilled. He took my hand and kissed it.

'I'll put it up on my bedroom wall,' he said.

The manager was touched. 'I'll save some posters for you,' he said. 'Keep coming to the Rialto.'

We assured him that we would keep coming.

Pablo kept me company on the way back to Barlowganj. It was dark by the time we reached the Hollow Oak gates. Pablo's mother was pacing up and down the garden path.

'Thank you for walking home with him,' she said, obviously relieved to see us. 'Sometimes he starts dreaming and gets lost. Would you like to come in?'

'Another time,' I said.

Ruskin Bond

'After the next picture,' said Pablo. 'You'll come with me, won't you?'

'If your mother agrees.'

'Pictures, pictures,' she said. 'That's all he lives for. And there are five cinemas in town!'

'But if you are on holiday, what does it matter?'

Pablo was so pleased to have an ally in me that he broke into Spanish as he said goodnight: *Buenas noches. Adios, amigo!*

8

There's just one way to write: put pen to paper and allow the words to come by themselves. As they will, if you don't interrupt and don't juggle them around too much.

In my window seat at Maplewood I allowed the words to come through the window, laden with the scents of summer. An old honeysuckle, planted by someone fifty or sixty years ago, climbed the outside wall and poured its heady fragrance into the room. I was the beneficiary of someone else's loving labour—a woman who loved gardens and planted and cared for this honeysuckle and watched it grow. And when she died, the garden too died of neglect; but the honeysuckle, being strong, was so well established against the wall that no one thought of cutting it down any more than they thought of pulling the house down. So there it was, adding its fragrance to the words as they floated in through the open window.

My good companion, the honeysuckle; that, and the babblers who often hopped in to snap up the moths that had knocked themselves out overnight, flinging themselves against the lighted window; that, and the little shrew, the *chuchunder*, who ran squeaking from room to room, weak sighted and rather helpless, expecting my protection from the questing tabby cat from across the road.

And one fine day there was Pablo at my door. Pablo bearing a gift.

He unrolled a poster, and there stood Laurel and Hardy, as large as life, in a film called *The Flying Deuces*.

'Saw it when I was a boy,' I said.

'It's being shown again. You said you liked Laurel and Hardy.'

'Stan and Olly forever!'

'It's showing tomorrow.'

'Then we'll see it together. How many posters do you have now?'

'Seven.'

'Mr Ahuja is very generous.'

'My mother sent him a cake.'

'Fair exchange.'

'But I have a problem, amigo.'

'What's that?'

'I can't put them up anywhere. Sister Clarissa is in charge while the Maharani is away and she says we can't have film posters stuck all over the walls. Not even in my room.'

'Mean old thing. A few posters would brighten up the place—better than having mounted tiger heads and deer antlers suspended from the walls. We should pull them all down!'

'We can hardly move about indoors, she's so fussy. Won't let us touch the furniture. Nothing must be moved. Nothing has been moved since the Maharaja died.'

'When does the Maharani come back?'

'Don't know. Sister won't say.'

'Doesn't your father phone?'

He shook his head. There was anger in his eyes—too much anger for so delicate a boy.

'My sister drew a picture of her,' he said, taking a folded sheet from his coat pocket.

'Of the Maharani?'

'No, of the nun.'

He straightened out the sheet and showed me a crude sketch of Sister Clarissa. It was quite a good likeness. Piercing, protruding eyes stared out of a long, cavernous face. There was a cruel twist to the mouth. One eye appeared to be higher than the other; perhaps Anna had got them out of alignment.

'I have never seen her so close up,' I said. 'There's something scary about her.'

'I heard the servants talking about her in the kitchen. They say she isn't really a nun. That's just a disguise.'

'Why would she dress up as a nun?'

'Because she's *wanted*,' said Pablo mysteriously.

'Wanted?'

'Wanted for murder.' He said this in a sort of stage whisper, although there was no one to hear us talking. 'I heard it from the old chowkidar. She

70

was a nurse, she worked in a big hospital, and if she thought one of the patients was a bad person, had done something wrong, she would come by whenever she was on night duty and *suffocate* them.'

'How?'

'With a pillow, of course.'

'You've seen too many movies, Pablo.'

'But I haven't seen it happen in a movie. The chowkidar, Ram Singh, knows all about her. He's been with the palace staff since he was a boy—first in Mastipur, now here. When they discovered she was killing sick people, she had to go into hiding. The Maharaja helped her. She was his aunt, a gypsy from Europe. He hid her in the palace for a year, and when she came out she was no longer a nurse—she was dressed as a nun!'

Pablo looked so serious, so worried, that I burst out laughing.

'But it's true,' he said. 'I'm afraid of her, amigo. She doesn't like us. We are in the way.'

∽

With my window open to the wind and the rain, I can recall that time, that summer of long ago, and

I see before me the pale, beautiful face of Pablo, his long fingers (more artistic than his sister's), the green of his eyes reflecting the morning sun, his soft, sensual lips, and one of those rare smiles which brought out the dimples in his cheeks.

With the rain on my face, I remembered the rain on our faces when we were caught in a sudden storm, walking back from the pictures to Barlowganj, no umbrellas, his futile efforts to keep his latest poster from getting wet. We stopped at the cottage and I wrapped him in a large towel, and he sat on my bed shivering while I made him a mug of strong coffee. He was an ugly duckling, all ribs and sharp bones, but with the promise of becoming a swan one day.

He smoothed out the poster and gazed tenderly at the sodden image of Elvis Presley—not exactly my poster boy, but a teenage heart-throb in his time.

'It will dry out,' I said.

He looked up and smiled at me—not with the same tenderness that he had bestowed on Elvis, but with the affection that comes from trust and companionship.

But to return to that morning in the window seat,

and the drawing of Sister Clarissa. Pablo had placed it on my desk—not much on it in those days—and he was staring at it with an expression far removed from the benevolent gaze which he had bestowed upon Elvis. A spasm of Latin fury swept across his face. It was gone in a moment, but I would remember it for a long time.

'She-devil!' he hissed, as he spat upon the image. 'Witch woman!' And picking up my paper knife he stabbed repeatedly at the face and figure of the crude representation of the nun.

'Well, that should do for her,' I said. 'And, by the way, you've broken my favourite paper-cutter.' It had broken off at the tip due to the violence with which Pablo had slammed it into the table.

'I'm sorry,' he said, quite contrite. 'I'll get you another.'

'Don't worry. A table knife will do just as well— though not for stabbing Sister Clarissa!'

I took the desecrated drawing, set a match to it, and watched it burn to cinders.

'And now she's been cremated,' I said.

Pablo clapped his hands with childish glee and planted a kiss on my cheek.

'I'll walk home with you,' I said.

It was a short walk through the woods to Hollow Oak. Birds and small animals were quite numerous in this patch of forest, but Pablo was no nature lover. He seemed ill at ease in this unfrequented stretch and was glad to be out in the open, on the bare hillside surrounding the estate.

'Are you coming in?' he asked at the gate.

'Only when H.H. is here.'

'My mother said we'll be renting a place for ourselves. Then you'll come?'

'Of course. Meanwhile, there's the old witch.'

Sister Clarissa was coming around the corner of the house. She did not look as though anyone had been stabbing her again and again. Her long, vigorous stride took her swiftly across the garden path. H.H.'s pekes danced at her heels, yapping at nothing in particular.

'Your magic did not work,' I whispered to Pablo. 'But keep trying.'

'You're late for lunch,' called the deep-voiced nun. 'Your mother was worried. Don't take off without telling us.'

Pablo gave me a wave and sauntered through the

gate. Sister Clarissa stared at me disapprovingly but said nothing, knowing I was a friend of Neena's.

Pablo gave me a conspiratorial look as I waved back. As much as to say, 'I haven't finished with her yet.'

9

Sometimes I couldn't help feeling that Neena's mission in life was to make life as unpleasant as possible for all those who had any claim on her purse or affections. And if they were dependent on her, she really applied the screws. It gave her a thrill to watch others dance to her tune. Even more of a thrill if they tripped and hurt themselves.

The boys received their allowances, but never quite enough to satisfy their longing for the good life, of which they'd had a taste and to which they felt they were entitled. They had been brought up to think of themselves as princes, and yet here they were, no better off than any teenager of modest means. They were incapable of self-employment or any employment. The younger one dropped out of school and took up with a bunch of drug addicts. He turned up from time to time, demanding money. H.H. always gave him enough to enable him to leave town. She'd washed her hands of him even before he was sixteen. Kartik, the older boy, was already a hopeless alcoholic. In his early twenties, he was a bed-wetter, barely capable of looking after himself. Neena maintained that they took after their father, and she may have been right; but she did nothing to help them straighten out their lives. The selfish streak that I had noticed in her when she was younger was now even more deeply embedded in her nature. Her own personal bank balance grew from stocks and shares and clever investments. If others were incapable of making money, then more fools they!

Neena was not smart enough to have become a politician, like some former royals who had made the transition quite successfully. Her views were so feudal, and she so outspoken, that political parties shied away from her. She believed in the old caste system, in the inequality of peoples and nations; she believed that the haves should have more than the have-nots. She was of the view that black people were inferior to fair people, and that there should be masters and servants, even a master race. She would have revived the slave trade had that been possible. There were probably a few people who agreed with her, but they were not so vocal about it.

Shunned by politicians and social activists, Neena gave her attention to diplomats and holy men. For the present, it was diplomats. But not the families of diplomats.

Mrs Montalban and her children were a nuisance, and H.H. wanted them out of the way—especially when dear Ricardo was in town. At the same time she wanted to have Ricardo visiting as often as possible. He was great in bed, and also a good provider of expensive wines, spirits and liqueurs. Neena liked the best, but she was no spendthrift. A diplomat had many uses.

Sister Clarissa was instructed to find a cottage for the family. The cottage was found, badly in need of repair and restoration. It would be at least a month before it could be occupied. As for school, it was already midterm and admissions were kept pending. Pablo's extended holiday would be extended even further.

He clapped his hands gleefully. 'You can teach me at home,' he said. 'You will be my tutor, all right? We will see lots of pictures!'

Most of my education had taken place in second-hand bookshops. It appeared that Pablo's was to take place in Mussoorie's cinema halls.

'We'll have to cut down on the pictures,' I said. 'More nature walks. That way you'll learn some geography, botany and arithmetic.'

'Geography, yes. Botany, yes. But arithmetic how?'

'By counting the number of seeds in a sunflower and comparing if with the number of seeds in a dandelion. Which has more?'

'I don't know, amigo.'

'Neither do I. So let's start looking for dandelions.'

∾

It was the beginning of innumerable walks. Sometimes they ended up at one of the cinemas, but most of the time we covered quite a lot of ground, taking in Cloud End, the Haunted House and the ruins of Colonel Everest's house, all at the hill station's extremities. Not many cars in those days, not many motorable roads either, so we did a lot of trudging, stopping at small inns and tea shops to sustain ourselves with boiled eggs, old buns and biscuits, and sweet, milky tea.

One day we ended up at an extensive cemetery, and I took Pablo down a winding path, in amongst old graves, some of them going back well over a hundred years. The lettering had worn off most of the slabs, but had lasted better on some of the more upright tombstones—most of them British graves from the colonial era.

Hundreds of graves—the city of the dead—all reminders of our frail hold on this life and the oblivion into which we must pass. The famous, the humble, the wicked, the innocent, the ancient, the infant, struck down at random, sometimes in the midst of a busy life, sometimes when it had hardly got started . . .

Sceptre and crown must tumble down
And in the dust be equal made
With the poor crooked scythe and spade.

I remembered these lines from a poem I'd learnt at school, but I couldn't remember the name of the poet. I spoke them aloud for Pablo's benefit, but he wasn't listening.

'This angel has lost her head,' he said, pausing in front of a small statue of a winged angel carved out of granite. The head was indeed missing. As were the heads and limbs of other statuary in the cemetery. Somebody had been collecting angels' heads. Even the odd wing!

'This one has only one wing,' observed Pablo, indicating another broken angel. 'How will she fly?'

'Angels were invented before aeroplanes,' I said. 'Now that everyone can fly, who needs angels? Science hasn't left us with much to believe in.'

Pablo sat down on the grass and said, 'I'm tired. What are you looking for, amigo?'

'Nothing,' I said. 'Just contemplating the void.'

'The void?'

'The emptiness. The futility of it all. The yearning, the struggle, the desire, the loving, the hating. And it all ends here, or on the funeral pyre. Dust or ashes.'

'*Finit. Kaput.*'

'You heard that in a movie.'

'Alan Ladd doesn't die.'

'He died last month.'

'But we can still see his movies.'

'True enough. There's immortality, after all, courtesy Hollywood. So enough of graves and worms and epitaphs, let's go to the pictures.'

We began climbing the steep path to the lychgate.

'Look, there's an empty grave,' said Pablo, indicating a newly dug entrenchment.

'They always keep one or two ready,' I said. 'So they don't have to dig one at the last moment.'

'Well, this one is for Sister Clarissa,' said Pablo.

'You seem very certain.'

'Very soon.'

'She looks healthy enough.'

He gripped me by the arm, and gave me an odd, intense look that I couldn't fathom. 'Something will happen, I'm sure of it.'

'Come, we'll go to the pictures. This place has a depressing effect.'

We saw *Butch Cassidy and the Sundance Kid*, and walked home singing *Raindrops keep falling on my head.*

A small crowd had collected in the palace garden. Another party, perhaps.

Mrs Montalban ran towards us, visibly upset. 'Something terrible has happened, something terrible.'

'Is the Maharani all right?' I was always expecting something awful to happen to her, in spite of her claim to possess nine lives.

'Not the Maharani, Sister Clarissa. She tripped and fell down the stairs.'

'Is she dead?' asked Pablo.

His mother nodded, and led us indoors. 'Fell all the way down. All the way to the bottom step. Broke her neck. The Maharani will tell you more.'

10

There wasn't much more to tell.

H.H. arranged the funeral, but balked at paying for an expensive coffin and settled for a cheap plywood box.

There was only one undertaker in Mussoorie. Coffins were not in great demand, as the Christian population had declined over the years, and the undertaker—Mistriji as we called him—really made his living as a carpenter, making cupboards, desks and box-beds to order.

A box-bed was very like a coffin, but bigger,

made to accommodate various household items that were not in regular use. You slept on top of the box-bed, opening it only when necessary. They were quite popular with some of the smaller hotels. Only recently a family had moved into a hotel room, settled down for the night, and then found that the box-bed wasn't properly closed. They sat on it and jumped on it, but they couldn't get the lid to fasten. So they opened it and found a dead person inside. He'd been left behind by the previous customers—strangled and then stuffed rather clumsily into the box-bed. The culprits were never traced.

Anyway, Mistriji made a cheap standard-size coffin for Sister Clarissa who was duly interred in the grand city of the dead—and that too, in the very grave that Pablo had indicated would be her last resting place.

A handful of people attended the last rites. There were just four of us fit enough to act as pall-bearers, and we had some difficulty lowering the coffin. At the last moment the cheap, frayed rope broke and the coffin landed in the cavity with a crash, splitting open and revealing its occupant, no longer in her habit and very unlike the menacing figure we had known.

There was nothing we could do about it, except cover the smashed coffin and its occupant with flowers, leaves and earth. As it was now monsoon time there was plenty of foliage at hand. We left it to the chowkidar to finish the job.

'You might at least have given her a better coffin,' I chided Neena as we trudged out of the cemetery.

'And who would have appreciated it?' countered H.H. 'She wasn't royalty, you know.'

'I thought she was related to your late husband.'

'No, just his nanny. Or something else.'

Outside the lychgate I collared Dr Bisht, our local GP.

'You did the post-mortem, doctor. Tell me. Was she really a woman?'

The good doctor took me aside and said, 'H.H. asked me not to talk about it. But since I know you to be the soul of discretion, I can tell you in confidence—she was *neither*. The perfect hermaphrodite.'

Pablo had not attended the funeral.

'Not for children,' his mother had said.

So he had spent the afternoon at the Rialto, watching an adult film. He met me on the way home. He had a poster too. *The Blue Angel.*

'Not for children,' I said.

'Have you seen it?'

'I saw the earlier version. Before you were born. It was much better.'

'Did you like the funeral?'

'No.'

'I told you, didn't I? I told you it would happen.'

'Yes, you did. But don't make any more predictions. I like you better without them.'

He gave me his most engaging smile and took me by the hand. 'You are a very nice man.'

'Thank you. And you are a very nice boy. Sometimes.'

'Gracias!'

11

H.H. back in town meant that Signor Montalban was back too, and for the convenience of all concerned it was decided that his family would move into the rented house selected for them. Pablo did not object to the move, as the house was nearer to the town and its cinemas. It meant that I would see less of them as my cottage was almost an hour's walk in the opposite direction.

Montalban's visits to Mussoorie to see his beloved were brief, and he spent more time at the Hollow Oak palace than at his wife's residence. H.H. threw a party whenever he was in town. Mrs Montalban, pleading indisposition, stayed away. I attended only one of them, a lugubrious affair which ended with Neena drinking too much and ending up, quite literally, under the table. In trying to extricate her, I too collapsed on the floor, and we ended up a tangle of arms and legs.

'Just like old times,' said Neena, subsiding into a sofa. 'I wish you had got to grips with me when we were a little younger.'

'I did try,' I said. 'But you were always as elusive as a shark. You were looking for other prey.'

'Well, you were rather dull. Always had your head in a book. But I hear you're quite friendly with that equally dull creature, Signora Montalban.'

'She likes books too,' I said. 'I lend her mine and she lends me hers.'

'How romantic. Like Elizabeth Barrett and Robert Browning, reading their poems to each other.'

'Bet you never read any of their poetry.'

'Yes, I did. At school, remember? "The Pied Piper of Hamelin". And you're a bit of a Pied Piper yourself. That boy follows you around everywhere.'

'Pablo. He needs a father. But his father doesn't

need him. Too busy elsewhere. Too busy mixing drinks.'

Montalban was doing just that—standing behind H.H.'s minibar, making drinks for her guests.

'Diplomatic duties,' I said.

'You're just jealous,' said Neena.

'And you're jealous of Elizabeth Barrett Browning.'

Neena gave a shriek of laughter, got up, and sat down on the floor again. This time I did not help her up, but left her to the attentions of a tall, strikingly handsome foreigner wearing a saffron robe. It turned out that he was an Anglo-German neophyte at an ashram up in the mountains. He was drinking apple juice.

∾

Mrs Montalban moved into her new abode without any fuss or bother, engaged a cook and a maidservant, and directed all her energies into caring for her children. In other words, she was the ideal Indian wife and mother.

So, while H.H. played the femme fatale and Montalban fancied himself a Valentino, Mrs Montalban was simply a homely bread-and-butter woman who busied herself baking cakes and cookies.

And she baked them well, as I discovered one afternoon when I dropped in at Pablo's invitation a week or two after they had moved into their new abode.

Already, the wide veranda looked like no veranda I had ever seen. The walls were festooned with film posters, all assiduously collected over the summer months. Apart from the manager of the Picture Palace, Pablo had made friends with the projectionist at the Rialto, the ticket seller at the Majestic, and the tea stall owner at the Jubilee—all of whom had gone out of their way to save posters for him. Partly it was due to his personal charm and friendly nature; partly due to his generosity with his mother's cakes and cookies.

And now, on my first visit to the rented house, I was taken from one poster to another as though I were the chief guest at a grand art exhibition—which is what it was, in a way. For here were the great stars of the sixties and earlier in some of their most famous roles. And Pablo, in a way, was a pioneer, for he had discovered that the film poster was an art form in itself, and I doubt if anyone, till then, had built up such a collection. He must have had close to a hundred posters. Not all were on the veranda wall. His favourites were in his bedroom. And when I went to the bathroom to ease myself, I found myself staring at a large poster of *It's a Mad Mad Mad Mad World*. And I had to agree with it.

It was little sister Anna's birthday.

A large cake stood on a table in the sunroom— a small sitting room with glazed windows. During the day it received the morning sun; at night, the rising moon. It was Anna's favourite room, and she liked to sit there and draw or paint until it grew dark.

I looked at some of her sketches—flower studies, trees, small animals—all quite charming but nothing out of the ordinary—until I came to a sketch of a face, just a line drawing, incomplete but in a way quite compelling; the face of a girl, pretty and vivacious, but a little old-fashioned, judging by the plaited hair and the ribbons.

'Who's this?' I asked.

'Just a girl I saw the other day. She looked at me over the gate and hurried away. It was raining.

I saw her again yesterday. She had her face pressed to the window. She looked very sweet, but shy like a gazelle—she had her face against the glass and she kept staring at me. That's how I remember her features so well. But when I got up to open the window, she ran off. Just disappeared! I hope she comes again. I'd like her for a friend.'

I was the only guest at that little birthday party. Mrs Montalban had met a number of people while staying at Hollow Oak, but they had all been Neena's friends; she hadn't hit it off with any of them. Her English was weak and her Hindi non-existent; she spoke to her children in Spanish. But she was aware of Pablo's growing affection for me and she was glad of any overtures of friendship towards her and her family.

Montalban was of course absent—out of town—away on a diplomatic mission to Thailand or Timbuctoo, and this time without H.H. for company.

The cake was splendid, full of good things like walnuts and raisins and cherries, and I have to confess that I consumed the lion's share; but I was always like that, a glutton for the good things in life—birthday cakes, books and a comfortable bed, all in that order. Mrs M and the children were delighted by my appetite, and Mrs M vowed to bake bigger and better cakes if I would come over more often. I promised that I would.

H.H. must have heard that it was Anna's birthday because presently one of her lackeys arrived with a large gift-wrapped parcel. When opened, it revealed an expensive doll, beautifully dressed, with what appeared to be real hair—glossy black tresses—done up in a coiffure. Anna stood it up on the table and it immediately broke into a chorus of 'Happy Birthday to you!'

We all clapped and Mrs Montalban sat down to write a thank-you note to Neena. She would have sent her some cake too, but for the fact that I had finished it.

Pablo was staring intently at the doll.

'It looks like the Maharani,' he said, a glint of the devil in his eyes.

'Even the voice is a bit like hers,' I added.

'It's a beautiful doll,' said Mrs Montalban. 'Especially the dress.'

'And the hair,' said Anna, stroking it gently.

The doll was put aside and Pablo produced a guitar and began strumming on it.

'I didn't know you could play the guitar,' I said.

'Only a little bit,' he said, and played a familiar tune which sounded a bit like *Jealousy*, a tango from an earlier time. The tune was perhaps a fitting prelude to what happened next.

There was a jingle of bells and a rickshaw pulled by two uniformed but barefooted young men pulled up at the gate, and out stepped H.H. in all her finery, looking very regal, albeit a little unsteady on her feet.

'A party without me,' she scolded, genuinely upset. 'Why didn't you invite me?'

'It was just the children,' said Mrs Montalban defensively.

'And I suppose you're Peter Pan,' said Neena, glaring at me.

'I thought I was supposed to be the Pied Piper,' I said. 'But I came accidentally. I didn't know it was Anna's birthday.'

Anna held up the doll. 'Thank you for the lovely doll, Maharaniji. It's very beautiful.'

'It's just like the Maharani,' said Pablo, straight-faced. 'Even the voice.'

Neena ignored him. She had been conscious of his resentment ever since she had seduced his father. It did not bother her. Spreading a little unhappiness was one of her chief pleasures.

'Well,' she said, hands on hips, a typical pose when she wanted to get her way. 'We're going to celebrate properly. No tea and cakes, just cakes and ale! I'm taking you out for dinner. We'll go to the Savoy! And you can come too, Pied Piper. A pity Ricardo isn't here, but you'll have to do as our escort or whatever.'

'Your friend in need,' I said. 'Always at your service.'

'Good. You can pay for the drinks.'

The rickshaw—the late Maharaja's personal rickshaw—was dismissed as it could only seat two. Rickshaws were on their way out and only a few remained in town. But there were now three taxis and we sent for one of them, a large Chevrolet which had seen better days. I sat up front next to the driver and H.H., and Mrs Montalban and the children squeezed in at the back.

It was late July, and a monsoon mist hung over the mountain. There were hardly any tourists in town

96

and the grand old hotel was practically empty; but the bar was functioning, or so it seemed, and Neena headed straight for it.

Like the rickshaw and the taxi and the royal house of Mastipur, the old hotel had also seen better days. A musty odour emanated from the worn carpets. Outside it was raining; but inside, the decorative plants were drooping from lack of water. If you sat on an easy chair in the lounge there was a strong possibility of a loose spring probing your rectum.

H.H. wasn't wasting time in the lounge. She headed straight for the bar. She barged through the swing doors and we were immediately assailed by the combined odour of stale beer, mildew and disintegrating cheese-and-tomato sandwiches.

Neena herded us into this chamber of horrors and called out, 'Barman, barman, beer for all!'

There was no response.

The room was empty and there was no one behind the bar.

'Perhaps it's a dry day,' I said. 'Or someone's death anniversary.'

'Shut up,' said Neena. 'There are no dry days in this town.' She peered over the bar counter, then let out a shriek of laughter. 'Maybe there's a death after all. Our bartender is well and truly pissed!'

True enough, the bartender was stretched out on the floor, snoring away, blissfully unaware of the arrival of customers. It was obvious he'd been helping himself to various liquors and liqueurs, trying each one for taste and aroma.

'He's completely blotto,' said Neena. 'We'll just have to help ourselves.' And she reached for a bottle of Scotch, intoning, 'Don't be vague. Ask for Haig.'

'A glass of wine for me,' interposed Mrs Montalban. 'The children can have soft drinks.'

'No soft drinks here,' said Neena. 'But Pablo can have a beer. My boys started when they were six.'

'And look at them now,' I said. 'Pickled for life.'

'No lip from you, Peter Piper. Down your whisky and then go in search of the manager. If you can't find the manager, find the cook. If you can't find the cook, find the *masalchi*. We want something to eat. It's Anna's birthday, damn and blast!'

Damned and blasted, I went in search of hotel staff and, after wandering around the empty halls and corridors of this vast mausoleum, finally bumped into someone who looked like a manager.

'We're looking for something to eat,' I said.

'Well, so am I, sir.'

'Are you the manager?'

'No, I'm the pianist.'

'Pianist! But I haven't seen a piano anywhere.'

'There isn't one. They sold it last week to a collector from Bombay. I'm Ivan Lobo,' he said, extending his hand.

We shook hands and I introduced myself.

'The hotel appears to be deserted,' I said. 'And the bartender is fast asleep.'

'Well, the hotel is up for sale, you know. The owner has gone missing—last seen in Bangladesh. And the cook is in hospital with food poisoning.'

'Well, in that case, I don't think we'll want anything to eat. I'd better go back to the bar and tell the others.'

'I'll come with you,' said Mr Lobo. 'Perhaps I can be of help.'

When we got to the bar, Neena was on her second whisky.

'Don't be vague,' she chirruped. 'Ask for Haig!'

'This is Mr Lobo,' I said. 'He's the pianist.'

'How lovely! It's just the sort of evening for some

romantic music. *What do they do on a rainy night in Rio?* I love that one.'

'Well, it's a rainy night in Mussoorie. And there's no piano. And no cook.'

'Well, fetch the owner. Isn't he around?'

'He's gone underground,' I said.

'Oh, it's old Chawla, I'm not surprised. Used to play billiards with my husband. Did nothing else. Have a drink, Mr Lobo. I've always had a soft spot for pianists.'

She poured Mr Lobo a Patiala peg and gave herself another. Meanwhile, the bartender had woken from his slumbers. He wiped his face on a table-cloth, burped, and asked us if we'd like something to drink.

'We're doing all right without you,' said Neena. 'But give yourself a drink, you poor man. You look as though you need one. And you'll probably be out of a job next week.'

'Now then, Melaram,' said Mr Lobo, expanding a little under the gentle influence of Haig. 'We have to do something for our guests here. Pull yourself together, run down to the bazaar, and order some food from the Hum Tum Dhaba. What would you like, madam?'

'Maharani, not madam.'

'A thousand pardons, Your Highness. I didn't know you were you. I've seen your picture in the papers. The Maharani of Ranipur.'

'Mastipur, sir. Mastipur.'

'Coming from Goa, I am unfamiliar with the names of so many of our old states.'

'So why aren't you playing the piano in Goa? Everyone there is a musician, I hear.'

'They were, until Jimi Hendrix died in his bathtub and Janis Joplin took an overdose. Singers get nervous when they reach the age of twenty-seven. That's when they succumb to something or the other.'

'Well, you're a pianist, not a singer. And if you're out of a job, you can come and play the piano for me every evening. It needs tuning anyway.'

'Much obliged, ma'am.'

'Maharani, *Ji.*'

'Your Highness.'

'That's better.'

Food was brought from the Hum Tum Dhaba (at Savoy prices) and the children and I tucked in. Mrs Montalban never ate much. H.H. concentrated on the whisky. And Mr Lobo, out of politeness, kept pace with us. The taxi having been dismissed, the bartender was sent out in search of another, but failed to return.

The evening had been too much for him.

The clock on the wall hadn't worked since the great earthquake of 1905, but my watch was showing midnight when the party broke up. Mrs Montalban and the children decided to walk home. Neena was by now incapable of walking. Mr Lobo and I got her as far as the front steps, where she subsided into a hydrangea bush.

'There's an old rickshaw kept in a shed near the office,' said Mr Lobo. 'I'll see if I can get someone to pull it for us.'

But at that late hour there was no rickshaw-puller to be found. I was still trying to extricate Neena from the hydrangea—and being roundly abused in the process—when Mr Lobo came round the corner, pulling at the decrepit but movable rickshaw.

'If you can get her in,' he gasped, already out of breath, 'we'll take her home ourselves!'

'He's a real man!' shrieked Neena. 'Not a namby-pamby bastard like you!'

'Any more abuse and I'll leave you here with Mr

Lobo. You can both occupy the VIP suite. Many famous people have slept in it—Emperor Haile Selassie, the Panchen Lama, Pearl S. Buck, Raj Kapoor, Helen, and Polly Umrigar.'

'What—all together?' giggled Neena. 'It must have been quite an orgy!'

'Not all together, Your Highness. Separately, and at different times.'

'Helen of Troy, too.'

'Not Helen of Troy. Helen the Bollywood dancer.'

'Well then, let's dance,' said H.H., making a great effort to get up. 'Mr Lobo can play the piano while we dance.'

'First we have to get you home. The piano's at your place, remember? The hotel doesn't have one.'

'When we're all out dancing cheek to cheek,' H.H. began singing an old Fred Astaire number.

Mr Lobo and I began singing along with her, at the same time getting her to stand up and stagger towards the rickshaw. We managed to get her on to the seat, where she sat up for a moment, observing, 'These two don't look like my rickshaw boys,' before subsiding again.

'You pull and I'll push,' said Mr Lobo gallantly.

'No, you pull and I'll push,' I countered. 'Pulling is better exercise for piano players. I'm just a pen-pusher.'

That settled, we set off on the long haul to Hollow Oak, and believe me, it was a struggle all the way. The rickshaw was an old one, long out of use. It squeaked and rattled, and the wheels gave every indication of wanting to come off. Nevertheless, we made progress, encouraged by cries of abuse alternating with shouts of merriment from H.H., who was obviously enjoying the ride.

For those few who were out on the Mall that night, it must have been quite a sight—Kipling's phantom rickshaw emerging from the mist on a moonlit night, propelled along by a couple of well-dressed but dishevelled gentlemen who were spurred on by a mad Maharani waving in royal fashion to an imaginary crowd—the effect spoilt only by the obscenities that tripped off her tongue.

We got her home eventually and put her to bed. I had the guest room opened for Mr Lobo and told him he'd better stay the night.

'About giving me a job as a pianist,' he said. 'Did she really mean it?'

'You'll know in the morning,' I said. 'Get a good night's sleep. And if she throws you out in the morning, you can come and have breakfast with me.'

12

Mr Lobo wasn't thrown out. His gift as a pianist must have been appreciated by H.H. because two or three evenings later, as I walked past Hollow Oak, I heard the tinkle of a piano and recognized the immortal strains of *When Irish eyes are smiling*, the only thing Irish about H.H. and Mr Lobo being the whisky they had obviously been drinking. It was Irish disguised as Scotch and bottled in Bijnor. Not from Ricardo's cellars.

They were duetting in a grand manner, à la Nelson Eddy and Jeanette Macdonald, and while Mr Lobo had a pleasing tenor voice, Neena's raucous strains took all the mystery out of *Ah! Sweet mystery of life.* Tender romance was not her forte.

I continued on my way, stopping at Mrs Montalban's for a mid-morning coffee. Here I learnt that Mr Montalban would be back in a few days, with the intention of spending some time with his family and of course 'our wonderful friend the Maharani'.

I found Pablo on the front veranda. He was holding Anna's doll—Anna's birthday doll, the one that supposedly resembled the Maharani—and he was busy sticking drawing pins into various parts of its anatomy.

'Drawing pins won't work,' I said. 'You need something with greater penetration.'

He wasn't put out by my intrusion.

'I've got a hammer and nails,' he said, his eyes lighting up. 'Or I could take out all the stuffing.'

'Anna wouldn't like that. Disembowelling her favourite doll.'

'It's not her favourite doll. She doesn't come near it. Actually, she's not into dolls. Prefers ghosts.'

'Ghosts?'

'She keeps seeing a little girl who wants to play with her.'

'Yes, she drew a picture of her. I thought it was just a girl she'd imagined. Have you seen her?'

He shook his head; a lock of hair fell across his brow, giving him a tender, innocent look. Not the sort who practises voodoo on dolls.

'Only Anna has seen her.'

'Perhaps she's a real girl, but very shy. And she runs away, like a frightened gazelle.'

'The old mali says the house is haunted.'

The old mali was an eighty-year-old gardener who did odd jobs at various houses on the hillside. According to him, all the old houses were haunted.

'And what else does he say? That someone died here in tragic circumstances. Most people die at home, you know. It would be hard to find an old house which hadn't been witness to a death or two. Why aren't hospitals haunted? People die in them every day.'

'My mother says some people like to return to their old homes from time to time. They won't go back to a hospital.'

'Don't blame them. Hospitals are scary places— even for ghosts.'

As the evening wore on, Pablo took out his guitar and began strumming it without actually settling into a tune.

'Play something simple,' I said.

And for the first time I heard him singing. It was an old lullaby—something out of Africa, I think. I put it down in words that I remember, for he sang it first in Spanish and then in English:

How can there be a cherry without a stone?
How can there be a chicken without a bone?
How can there be a baby with no crying?
How can there be a story with no ending?

And then the answer to this gentle riddle:

A cherry when it's blooming, it has no stone,
A chicken when it's hatching, it has no bone,
A baby when it's sleeping has no crying . . .
A story of 'I love you' has no ending . . .

'You sing better than you play,' I said. 'You must sing more often.'

He began singing softly in Spanish and presently

we were joined by Anna and Mrs Montalban. She poured me a glass of red wine and placed a currant cake before me. Normally I wasn't a wine drinker, but it went well in that house and in that company.

The sun went down with a lot of fuss. First a fiery red, and then in waves of pink and orange as it slid beneath the small clouds that wandered about on the horizon. The brief twilight of northern India passed like a shadow over the hills, and dusk gave way to darkness. I had stepped outside to watch the sunset. Now a lamp came on in the sitting room, followed by the veranda light. An atmosphere of peace and harmony descended on the hillside.

Pablo was calling me. 'Amigo, come quickly. Pronto, pronto!' Whenever he was excited, he broke into Spanish.

I stepped back into the room to find him pointing at the far wall.

A faint glow had spread across the whitewashed wall, as though a part of that spectacular sunset had been left behind. And emerging from this suffused light, as through a rent in the clouds, was the face of a girl. Old-fashioned, sad–happy, beautiful.

'It's her!' exclaimed Anna. 'I've seen her at the window sometimes. And now she's *inside*!'

'She means no harm,' said Mrs Montalban, as composed and unruffled as always. 'She wants to be back here, she longs to be with us—a happy family!'

And it *was* a happy family, in Montalban's prolonged absence.

But the face on the wall soon faded, returned to its own eternal twilight. Who was she, and why had she come back? Perhaps Mrs Montalban was right, and she longed to be of this world again.

We would never know—until and unless we joined her.

13

Next day, when the children spoke to the old mali about the apparition, he looked gloomy and said it was a warning of bad times to come.

'At this time of the year there is much evil in the air. Fog and damp and leaf mould rotting. Even the plants don't like it. They are longing for a little sunshine.'

'So are we,' said Mrs Montalban.

We had put up with over two months of monsoon rain and we were all longing for blue skies.

And of course something did happen to break the

monotony; although, as the old mali had predicted, it came with the suddenness of a flash flood.

Mr Montalban returned a little earlier than expected.

Nothing extraordinary about that, for he came and went as he wished, being his own master to a certain extent.

He was a hot-blooded man, obsessive about his possessions—his family (which he took for granted), his wife (whom he practically ignored, so confident was he of his dominance), and his mistress, Neena, whom he was beginning to take for granted too.

Even though I was a regular visitor at his family's home, he did not for a moment suspect his wife of any infidelity; nor had he reason to do so. I liked her for her modesty and homeliness. I liked the children; I had a special relationship with Pablo. Montalban ignored me. He did not see me as a threat. Even in his relationship with Neena, he did not view me as a rival. Neena and I had been friends from our schooldays. That, somehow, nullified any physical attraction we might have had for each other.

So when he returned to Mussoorie he dropped off his luggage at his house, along with the presents he had brought for his children, presented me with a bottle of wine (I happened to be on the premises); declared that he felt like a walk; and set off in the direction of Hollow Oak, fully confident that he was master of that house too and that a royal welcome would be awaiting him.

Indeed, he would have been welcomed with open arms had Neena been prepared for his return. Easily bored, and restless during his absence, she had looked around for other diversions, and had found one in the person of Mr Lobo.

Mr Lobo was a good little pianist, and there was also an amorous side to his nature. Neena's piano lessons went on till late at night and ended in the early hours. Sometimes they began again in the afternoon. From the music room to the bedroom it was only a few steps. And when it suited her, Neena could move with the speed of a Usain Bolt, or a bolt of lightning.

Naughty Neena, she must have known it was a bit risky, since all the servants know exactly what was going on. And in a small town, prone to gossip, exaggeration and fabrication, 2+2 equals 22.

Ricardo Montalban strode into Neena's bedroom just as she and Mr Lobo were getting ready for a nocturnal musical session. It wasn't very late, but piano lessons were over and an early supper had been washed down with some excellent Bordeaux wine (supplied at an earlier date by Ricardo Montalban), and Mr Lobo was about to demonstrate his prowess with the baton rather than the piano when he caught a glimpse of Ricardo framed in the doorway.

Mr Lobo had not seen Ricardo before, and mistaking him for another of H.H.'s lackeys, said, 'We'll ring if we need another bottle'—words calculated to inflame the passions of any jilted lover, let alone a hot-blooded Spanish diplomat.

A revolver appeared quite suddenly in Ricardo's hand, and he was pointing it straight at Mr Lobo's heart.

And how did Mr Lobo respond?

He did what any sensitive musician would have done in the circumstances. He had a heart attack.

Even as he clutched his chest and opened his mouth in a silent scream, Neena emerged from the bed sheets, half tipsy but in fine fettle, and screamed at Montalban to get out of the room and head for South America.

Montalban pointed the gun at H.H. She responded by picking up a bottle of tomato sauce and flinging it at him. A terrible waste of Crosse & Blackwell's. Even as the bottle bounced off his shoulder, splattering his shirt front with sauce, the revolver went off, the bullet embedding itself in a portrait of his late Highness which hung above the bed. At the same time two pekes ran in from the bathroom, barking furiously and snapping at Ricardo's legs.

This was when I came in.

Anticipating trouble, I had been following Montalban at a discreet distance; and now, hearing a revolver shot, I dashed up the stairs to witness this strange tableau in H.H.'s bedroom.

Mr Lobo was on his back, his legs convulsing, a gurgling sound issuing from his throat. H.H. was still swearing at Ricardo, and the pekes were having a party of their own, now snapping at poor Mr Lobo, whose convulsions appeared to have upset them more than the gunshot.

Always level-headed when it was someone else's

emergency, I took the gun from Ricardo and slipped it into my pocket. I then went to the phone and telephoned for Dr Bisht.

He lived nearby, and within a few minutes I heard his scooter coming up the driveway. A servant brought him into the room. He looked around, saw tomato sauce splattered all over Ricardo's shirt front, and assuming it was blood, made straight for the diplomat, who did indeed look pale and somewhat subdued.

'Not him, you fool!' shouted Neena. 'That's just tomato sauce. The one on the bed. My pianist's had a heart attack.'

Mr Lobo had stopped convulsing but he was still in bad shape. Dr Bisht made a quick examination, looked troubled, and said we should get the patient to hospital.

'Will he live?' asked Neena.

'Can't say,' said Dr Bisht, never one to make a hurried prognosis.

'Well, we can't have him dying in my bed. Just think of the scandal! So what are you staring at, all of you? Get him to the hospital, you idiots!'

Encouraged by the pekes snapping at our heels,

we carried Mr Lobo downstairs, got him into H.H.'s old Daimler, and drove him to the mission hospital. That is, Ricardo drove while the good doctor and I sat in the back seat with the expiring Mr Lobo.

14

Mr Lobo did not expire. His symptoms had been more alarming than his condition warranted. Confronted by a jilted rival in love flourishing a revolver, many of us would have had a similar reaction.

Sedated and placated, Mr Lobo soon felt better. But he decided to remain in hospital for a few days. He felt safer there. He had no intention of returning to the perils of giving piano lessons to Neena. And at the uninhabited Savoy he would have no protection. He felt reasonably secure in the private ward that had been paid for by H.H. He lingered there for a week. H.H. did not visit him, but she sent him hampers of food, toiletries, magazines and several pairs of pyjamas. She also bought his rail ticket, first-class air-conditioned, to Bombay. And if he wanted a job, well, there was that hotel in distant Pondicherry, and she would convince the management of their need for a pianist.

'You can see him off, Ruskin,' said Neena, squeezing my arm in a sisterly fashion. 'I rely on you in these matters. What are friends for, after all? Take the Daimler, and make sure you put him on the Bombay Express. I don't want any more fireworks around here.'

So I took the Daimler, picked up Mr Lobo from the hospital, drove him down to Dehra Dun, and saw him off on the Bombay Express. He seemed happy to be going home.

Returning to Mussoorie, I was told by the servants that H.H. was drunk and in a foul mood. So I parked the Daimler and walked home. She could thank me another day.

∾

And of course it was time for the Montalbans to leave. Ricardo's affair with Neena was definitely over. That shot fired in anger had been his mistake. And Mr Lobo had been Neena's mistake. So they were quits and free to go their own ways and have as many lovers as they pleased.

'We are leaving next week,' said Mrs Montalban, informing me of their impending departure. 'It has nothing to do with H.H. My husband has a new posting in Jakarta, and the children will go to school there. The children will miss you, dear friend. They have grown quite fond of you. Especially Pablo. Tell him you will visit us in Jakarta.'

I couldn't see how I was going to visit them in Jakarta or anywhere else, my funds being particularly low at the time; but Pablo, with all the optimism of youth, seemed convinced that we would meet again. Financial constraints did not figure in his life, and probably never would; his father was in the diplomatic service, and his mother came from a wealthy, aristocratic background. It occurred to me that Montalban had, in fact, received good postings due largely to her wealth and influence. A plain woman she might have been, but she had the whip hand and knew full well that his amorous adventures were no more than interludes. There was no way he was going to leave her.

So our parting was not a sentimental one. The children were excited at the prospect of living in a different country. Mussoorie was, after all, a dull sort of place, unless you happened to like walking in the hills or consuming ice creams on the Mall.

Still, Pablo showed his genuine regard for me by making me a present of all his film posters.

The day before they left, the old mali came down the path to my cottage with a large bundle containing nearly all the posters Pablo had collected—some fifty to sixty posters, all neatly folded and well preserved. I put them away in a cupboard. I wasn't going to turn my cottage into the foyer of a cinema hall. But I was touched by the gesture. I knew that he treasured his collection—and he felt that they would be safe with me. So Marilyn Monroe, John Wayne, Elizabeth Taylor, Hema Malini and Meena Kumari all found their way into my cupboard—and were to remain there, untouched, for several years.

It was hard to tell just what H.H. felt about the departure of the Montalban family. Ricardo had left early, still in a mighty huff; the family was to pack up and follow.

When, on one of my walks, I met Neena outside her gate, she seemed terribly upset.

'Cheer up,' I said. 'You'll soon find other friends and admirers.'

'Shut up, you idiot,' was her response. 'I'm not concerned about those Mexicans leaving.'

'Bolivians.'

'Whatever. I'm upset because I've lost one of my dogs. One of the servants took them out for a walk early this morning, and a leopard sprang out from the bushes and carried off poor little Lao-tze.'

This was the first good news of the day, but all I said was, 'Too bad. It couldn't have been much of a meal. Merely an aperitif. But you've still got his partner, Ming-ling.'

'Ming-ling is grieving. She won't eat anything.'

'Wait till she gets her teeth into someone's calf. Dr Bisht is still limping.'

'You have no heart, Ruskin.'

'On the contrary, I'm all heart. And that leopard will be around again, looking for another snack. Nothing like a succulent little peke. So please keep

Ming-ling securely locked up. Don't let her out for a few days—preferably weeks. Better still—why not send her away to your palace in Mastipur? She'll be safe down there. No leopards in Mastipur.'

'Only hyenas.'

'Hyenas don't eat pekes. It's like dog eating dog.'

Neena gave me a quizzical look. 'You really are concerned, aren't you, Ruskin?'

'Poor little Lao-tze,' I said. 'I shall miss him.' And God forgive me for being such a liar, I might have added.

∿

Departure day arrived, and I joined the Montalbans in the taxi that took us down to the railway station in Dehra. Seeing people off was becoming a habit.

I had known the Montalbans for just over a year, but I was already feeling a part of the family. Those who have no family of their own soon grow attached to welcoming families, no matter how imperfect they may be. One has to belong somewhere. But families were always going away and leaving me behind.

I did not think I would see Pablo again, but I

put on a brave face, held his hand, and bade him a cheerful goodbye.

'See you in Jakarta,' I said. 'Or even in La Paz.'

He murmured the last line of his little song, 'A story of "I love you" has no ending,' and kissed my hand. The train drew out, and he vanished from my life.

I returned to Mussoorie, to its maniacal man-eater, the rich Maharani of Mastipur.

15

After the Montalbans' departure, I was feeling listless, uneasy. I had put down an anchor, but the ship had sailed off anyway. I liked being moored to one place; a houseboat person, not a yachtsman. Tranquil waters were preferable to stormy seas. But there were very few who could put down their anchor in the same way.

I was also keen to escape from H.H. for a while.

I spent the winter in Delhi, exploring old tombs and monuments and writing articles for the Sunday papers. The small fees I received helped me to pay for the tiny room I had rented in a guest house just behind Connaught Place. Summer too passed in this manner. Then the next year.

Sometimes I ate at a small café on a side street. The food was very ordinary, and the place wasn't popular, but that meant I had a table and a corner to myself at almost any time of the day. I lived on hamburgers and coffee for about a year, and gave myself a peptic ulcer.

One evening, while I was in my corner sipping coffee and making notes for a story on the history of Chandni Chowk, a couple of smartly dressed young women walked in and took the table next to me. They ordered tea and pakoras before noticing me in my gloomy corner.

'Why, it's Ruskin!' exclaimed one of them, who looked slightly familiar. Dimpled, bobbed hair, pink toenails. I couldn't quite place her.

'You came to our school sometimes, to see a play or a concert. I teach English in the junior school. My name's Sheela. I'm a cousin of your friend the Maharani, but she doesn't bother with us—we work for a living.'

'I remember you now,' I said politely but untruthfully. 'You must be having your holidays.'

'That's right. Two and a half months with nothing

to do. Super! So I'm off to Nepal to stay with friends. This is my sister Leela.'

Sister Leela bit into a chicken sandwich. 'Hello,' she said, her mouth full. 'Pleased to meet you.' And she took no further part in the conversation, concentrating all her energies on demolishing an entire plate of sandwiches.

Sheela, more diet conscious, sipped her tea and said, 'We haven't seen you around for some time.'

'I haven't been up to Mussoorie. I've missed two summers. Have I missed much?'

'Don't think so. The old Savoy hotel burnt down.'

'Poor old Savoy. No one died, I hope.'

'No. But they found two skeletons in the cellar.'

'Anything else?'

'The headmaster of Tara Hall shot himself. Nobody knows why. He'd been there for forty years.'

'That's probably the reason.'

'You sound so cynical. Let me think of some good news.'

She thought hard and long, but there wasn't much in the way of good news to pass on. Her companion ordered more pakoras, and offered me one. I accepted graciously.

Sheela brightened up. 'Oh yes! Your friend, the Maharani—but you must be in touch with her?'

'Long out of touch. But what has she been up to?'

'She's always up to something, isn't she? Well, last summer she was into religion, and the place looked like an ashram, with babas and godmen and their followers all over the place. There were rumours that she was going to take sanyas in the mountains and gift the palaces to her favourite guru. But which guru? There was some competition for the honour. Because the Mastipur palace was also involved. A valuable property. There were some who felt it was ideal for the purposes of meditation and mental wellness; others who felt it should be a centre for yoga in its physical form.'

'And what did the Maharani decide?' I asked, intrigued by all of this. I had never known Neena to meditate or contemplate or even cogitate. And as for yoga, she wasn't the sort to tie herself into knots or stretch her body to its limits. But who was I to judge? Perhaps she had a mystical nature beneath her sensual exterior.

'Is she still drinking?' I asked.

'Not openly. But she takes a nightcap regularly. Quite a large one.'

'You are well informed, Sheela.'

'Mussoorie's a small place. And Barlowganj even smaller.'

'So she hasn't decided yet?'

'Oh, she decided months ago. Threw them all out. With a little help from Brigadier Baghpat.'

'Who's he? Don't know him.'

'The new man in her life. She met him on the way to Badrinath. He took her to the Mana Pass and they fell in love. When they got back to Mussoorie he took over the management of her affairs, and there was an end to all talk of ashrams and health farms. He's moved into Hollow Oak, and they plan to turn the Mastipur palace into a luxury hotel.'

'Is he retired or still in the army?'

'Only just retired. A bit paunchy. Droopy moustache. She's quite fond of him. Calls him her Bugger-dear.'

'The Brigadier stands for that?'

'Oh, he dotes on her. Waits on her hand and foot. Does all her odd jobs—even keeps her sons away; they are always scrounging off her. And I think she's making a will, leaving one of the properties to him. So my lawyer friend tells me.'

'Lawyers are great gossips. And over the years

she's always been making wills. I've witnessed at least two. She'll make another next year, when she tires of the Brigadier. Or her sons get rid of him. They're desperate characters, I hear . . . I wonder if she insured her jewellery?'

'Don't know about that. But she's a queen, even if retreaded. Must have some jewellery.'

'Lots of it. Rubies and pearls. Emeralds and diamonds. Opals. Sapphires. I had a glimpse once, when she was showing off. Don't know where she keeps them, though.'

'In a safe-deposit box, probably.'

'No, she doesn't trust banks. Somewhere in Hollow Oak. Hidden away.'

'In some *hollow*,' said Sheela thoughtfully. 'In the hollow of a tree?'

'Someone might find them there. In a hollow of the mansion. Under the floorboards, probably.'

Sheela clapped her hands. 'How exciting! The treasures of Mastipur.' Sister Leela wasn't listening. She had ordered a hamburger and was attacking it with some ferocity. I had to admire her single-mindedness. Better to have a hamburger in hand than a diamond in dreamland.

131

'Where are you staying?' I asked.

'Don't know as yet. We left our bags at the station.'

'I'll help you find a place.'

When Leela had finished eating, we left the restaurant and went in search of a hotel room in the CP area. It was the tourist season and all the hotels were full.

'Never mind,' said Sheela. 'We'll sleep at the station and take a taxi to the airport early in the morning. The flight's at eight.'

'You can stay with me,' I said impulsively. 'I've got a room nearby. You two can sleep on the bed and I'll put a mattress on the floor for myself.'

Friends and relatives of the guests were constantly in and out of the guest house, with the result that the caretaker was never too sure about who was tenant, guest, casual visitor or stranger. Such places were rare, but they did exist in some parts of Delhi.

I took the sisters out to dinner, and Leela did full justice to the chicken sizzler and a chocolate sundae. Then we collected their bags and I brought them home in a taxi. All this had set me back about a thousand rupees. No holiday in Kathmandu for me!

Leela and Sheela made themselves at home in my room. Very sportingly, they slept on the floor, having first removed the Dunlopillo mattress from my bed. Normally I'm a good sleeper but plywood isn't the ideal surface on which to enjoy a good night's sleep. Even with the lights out, the girls kept chatting away till past midnight. I slept fitfully, dreaming one of my repetitive 'travel' dreams, in which I arrive in a foreign country having lost my money and my passport and end up in jail.

I woke to the sound of moaning and groaning from ground zero. My watch showed 2 a.m. Presently I became aware of someone climbing into bed with me. It was sister Leela. Was she a sleepwalker, or was she just uncomfortable on the floor?

She wasn't sleepwalking, she was cuddling up to me. Her full breasts were pressed against my palpitating chest, and her lips were exploring mine. Who was I to resist such a voluptuous creature?

I kissed her lightly, put my arm around her waist, drew her towards me. She put her lips to my ear. She was whispering something.

'What is it, sweetheart?' I asked.

'I'm hungry,' she said, loud enough to wake the dead.

I sat up with a start. The beautiful moment had passed. There was to be no frantic lovemaking at two in the morning. Instead, a picnic.

I got up, switched on the light, and went to the larder.

'Is there something to eat?' asked Leela hopefully.

'I'll do my best,' I said.

'You're so kind. I could kiss you.'

'You already have.'

I found some eggs and several buns. I fried an egg and made her a bun-omelette. Leela gobbled it up.

Sheela was now wide awake, demanding her share of this predawn breakfast. I made her a bun-omelette too.

'It's super,' said Leela, licking her lips. 'Can I have another?'

I made her another bun-omelette. I made one for myself too. I was getting to be quite good at it.

Two hours and several bun-omelettes later, the girls were ready to leave for the airport. I retrieved my mattress and returned to dreamland. Arriving in a foreign land, I was met by H.H. holding out a pari of handcuffs.

16

Three years slipped by quickly, enlivened only by another brief visit from sisters Sheela and Leela, who took advantage of my hospitality on their way to Goa. They were always going somewhere during their holidays. And I was always stuck in one place, struggling to survive on an invisible income.

I was becoming quite fond of the sisters. Their youth and vitality made me feel ten years younger when I was with them. Sheela was the more attractive; she took care of herself, had the figure of a tennis player and the looks of a Far Eastern movie star. Leela was chubby, which was only to be expected in view of her voracious appetite, but she was not ungainly or obese. I think she lost weight simply by trying to keep up with her more athletic sister.

It had been over a year since they last met me, and they brought me the latest Mussoorie gossip; also a letter from Dr Bisht.

I should have mentioned that when I left Mussoorie I had given up the cottage and kept some of my things with the good doctor, who had let me use one of his storerooms. Now he wanted the room in order to expand his dispensary. I told the girls about my problem, and Sheela told me not to worry, she'd collect my stuff (books and files and those posters of Pablo's) and look after it until I could come and collect everything.

Grateful for their help, I took them to dinner at the Imperial, blowing a month's earnings on a sumptuous meal. Leela drooled over the menu, ordering kababs and a tandoori chicken for herself. Sheela, to my relief, ordered spaghetti in tomato sauce. I settled for fish and chips. When the waiter brought us the wine list I looked at the price and shuddered. Fortunately for my pocket and my peace of mind, the girls said they didn't touch alcohol. I suggested mulligatawny soup, praising its health-giving properties, and looking up at the waiter I said, 'It's a speciality of the house, isn't it?'

'If you say so, sir,' he responded, without batting an eyelid.

'Thank you, Jeeves,' I said with feeling.

Actually, the dinner went off quite well, and the mulligatawny soup brought forth a flood of Mussoorie gossip.

'And how is the Maharani's Brigadier?' I asked casually.

'Dead,' said Sheela just as casually.

It took me two or three spoonfuls of mulligatawny soup to get over my surprise.

'Already? What was it—a heart attack? Neena needs a battalion, not a lone brigadier.'

'No dear, it wasn't that. She was very fond of the old soldier. But making her will in his favour did it for him.'

'The expectation of so much wealth may have been too much for him. His blood pressure must have shot up.'

'Nothing like that. He was run over by a car.'

'Bad luck. Neena must have been devastated.'

'She was very upset,' said Sheela, tucking into her spaghetti. (Leela had by now begun her assault on the chicken.) 'Especially so because the driver of the car happened to be her younger son, Karan.'

I almost choked on a potato chip. 'Well, well,' I said. I couldn't think of anything else to say. 'Well, well . . . And how did it happen? Purely an accident, of course.'

Leela looked up from her chicken, now sadly diminished, and spoke one word, *'Impurely,'* with emphasis, before resuming her nourishment.

'It happened in Dehra,' said Sheela. 'The Brigadier had been shopping in Astley Hall. He had just bought some flowers for the Maharani. A bouquet of red roses and a bunch of gladioli. He was crossing the road, arms full of flowers, to get to his car on the opposite side, when another car came down the road, going very fast. It struck the Brigadier and sent him flying. His head hit a lamp post. He lay there in a heap, all covered with flowers. The shopkeepers knew him and took him to the military hospital, but he was already dead.'

'And the car, didn't it stop?'

'Not at first. But further on, it went out of control and ended up against the park railings. Prince Karan was at the wheel. He was drunk, of course. He was locked up, but released the next day. Said the Brigadier wasn't looking when he walked across the road.'

'H.H. must have been very upset.'

'Didn't stop drinking for a week. Declared that Prince Karan wouldn't get a rupee when she died.'

'More wills in the offing. Well, let's hope there are no more accidents.'

'You stay away from her, my friend. Those two sons of hers are no good. They might think you are one of her lovers. They'll do anything to get their hands on her money. And as soon as she's dead, they'll sell all her properties.'

Dinner over, we stepped out into a chilly December night. Delhi was getting its winter rain and a light drizzle swept across the city.

'Where are you staying?' I asked the girls.

'With you, of course. Where else?'

17

Lights! Camera! Action!

Hollow Oak was a hive of activity. Early evening, and there were people all over the place: some in colourful costumes, some in jeans and T-shirts, some in formal dinner suits. Someone was calling out instructions on a megaphone, his voice drowned out by the shrill barking of several Pomeranians. The entire scene reminded me of a childhood nursery rhyme:

Hark, hark, the dogs do bark,
The beggars are coming to town.

Some in rags and some in bags,
And some in velvet gowns!

I had returned to Mussoorie after several years, had taken a gentle stroll down to Barlowganj, and found Hollow Oak to be the location for a Bollywood film. I was feeling a little depressed. In my extended absence, my manuscripts and papers had suffered from damp, leaking roofs and the depredations of rats. Most of the damage had occurred while they were in the good doctor's keeping; he'd been far too busy to check on their condition.

Pablo's posters had been eaten through or had simply rotted away. Just recently I had read that old film posters were being bought at fabulous prices by collectors in the USA. A fortune had been disintegrating in the doctor's godown. My fault entirely; I should have retrieved them much earlier. But fortune was always eluding me. And H.H. was always asking me to witness her wills—a sure sign that I was not a beneficiary!

One poster did survive in a reasonably good condition—Hitchcock's *Vertigo*—and I was tempted to put it up on the wall of my bedroom, as a sort of tribute to Pablo. But realizing that it would soon become prey to fish ants, I folded it up and put it away in a trunk.

I was now living in a different part of town, some distance from Hollow Oak, but I was still a good walker, and it was early October, a month when the hill slopes are showing off their post-monsoon foliage in a variety of hues—dahlias gone wild, in shades of mauve, magenta and startling red; tall cosmos swaying in the breeze; wild geranium tucked away among the ferns; asters flourishing on retaining walls; and bronzed chrysanthemums vying for attention with massive marigolds. Gardens both natural and man-made are at their best in the brief autumn before Diwali. This is what always draws me back to the hills.

Good weather brings in visitors, including moviemakers, and every autumn there are one or two films being shot on location in and around Mussoorie. In the old days they set up studio at the Savoy, but after it burnt down they had to look elsewhere, and it was not surprising that they should have been attracted to the spacious lawns and chalet-type architecture of Hollow Oak. And of course H.H. would have extracted a huge amount of money from the producers, who would also have been expected to replenish her bar on a daily basis, with the best single malts and other life-enhancing liquors and liqueurs.

Once the evening's shooting was over, the bar came to life, closing only at two or three in the morning when the revellers were more dead than alive.

And what of the film? It was a big production, and there were stars and starlets, supporting players, directors and assistant directors, cameramen and clapboard boys, make-up artistes, costumiers, consultants of all kinds, and lurking on the fringes a producer who looked as though he was convinced that he was about to lose a fortune. And he was probably right.

Into this cauldron I wandered that day, and was promptly mistaken for the catering manager. I suppose I looked like one.

'Where's the canteen?' asked a bright young starlet, exhibiting a large expanse of midriff. 'I haven't eaten since breakfast.'

'That's why you have such a good figure,' I said by way of flattery, but she did not look amused.

'Never mind my figure, I'm starving.'

143

'If you follow that man with the bulging waistline, you'll find the canteen.'

'But that's our star, Nasha Naveen.'

'Well, he's not wearing his waist-constrictor today. What's your name?'

'Lily.'

'Nice name. You'll go far with it.'

A flashy young man in below-the-knee shorts grabbed her by the arm. He had hairy legs and splayed feet. Another leading man, no doubt.

'Come on, Lily, help me rehearse my lines,' he said, and led her away; he looked back and gave me an unfriendly stare. 'Aren't you with the make-up crew?'

'Catering manager,' I said. 'Eat well, sleep well, live well. We look after your well-being. For beautiful feet try spaghetti with meat.'

He hurried away, probably thinking I was an escaped lunatic.

They were shooting a scene under the horse chestnut tree. The female lead was singing very badly (she'd be dubbed later no doubt) while she cavorted round the tree, followed by a lascivious-looking fellow who was the hero's rival in love. It being October, the chestnuts were ripe and ready to fall. One did fall. It struck the randy anti-hero on the bridge of the nose and brought him to a halt.

'That's the second time I've been hit by a chestnut. Must we shoot under this tree?'

'The script calls for it,' said the director, who was making his first film (he was the producer's brother-in-law). 'Let's give it another try.'

They did another take, and this time a chestnut struck the heroine on her ample bosom, disappearing down her blouse. She gave a shriek, presumably of distress (although it may have been of delight), and did a little jig, but to no avail; the chestnut had vanished.

'Now that's a trick worthy of the great Mustafa Pasha,' I said, referring to a magician of yore. 'A great scene. Keep it for the film.'

Everyone stared at me.

'And who do you think you are?' asked the leering anti-hero.

'Yes, who are you?' asked the director.

'Catering manager,' I said, and made my escape while they were gathering fallen chestnuts.

∾

I found H.H. on her back veranda, sipping a Bloody Mary. She had put on a little weight, and her hair was quite grey, but she had lost none of her bounce, her vivacity. Three hysterical Poms emerged from behind her easy chair and darted at me, snapping at my heels. Very gently, I kicked them away.

'How dare you assault my little ones!' shouted Neena. 'I'll report you to People for Animals. Now sit down and have a drink. Where have you been all these years?'

'Here and there. Making a living.'

'How terribly boring. You should have married me—then you'd have been rich.'

'I could have put up with your lovers,' I said, 'but not with your dogs.' And fended off another counter-attack from the Poms, who had replaced pekes as her favourite breed.

'Have you come to see me, or to take part in this film they're shooting on my property?'

'I know nothing about the film. Saw all this activity from the road, and thought the mob had taken over the palace as in the French Revolution.'

'My head's too beautiful to be chopped off.'

'So was Marie Antoinette's. Didn't someone steal the basket in which it fell?'

'You're the storyteller.'

'How much are those film people paying you?'

'What makes you think they're paying me anything?'

'Your charitable works don't extend to Bollywood. It must be a good amount. And most of it in black.'

'Go away, you horrible man. Why have you come back after so long? I heard you were starving somewhere on the outskirts of Delhi. Those girls kept me informed.'

'And you didn't think of sending me a money order.'

'Didn't have your address. No, don't go. Pour yourself a drink. I want to talk to you about my will.'

I poured myself a drink. There was no one else to pour it.

'Kartik is a helpless drunk. And the other boy— he's a criminal. I don't want them inheriting my money, or my property, or my jewels.'

'Give it all to me.'

'What a waste that would be. You'd go through it in a year.'

'Six months. I'd go to Timbuctoo, Honolulu and Kalamazoo; I'd go to South America and look up the Montalbans.'

'Don't mention them to me. Just pour me a small drink. Then we'll watch them shooting this awful film. And listen to me. I'm not so mean and I'm still quite fond of you. I'll leave you something in my will on one condition.'

'What's that?'

'You'll have to look after my dogs.'

I spilt vodka all over my trousers.

'What a horrible suggestion. You know I dislike dogs—especially the yapping, snapping breeds that you favour. I don't think you'll find anyone to keep them. Not for all the pearls in the world.'

'Hans will take care of them. I'll leave him the property. He'll look after Hollow Oak and the dogs. Let's go and look at the stars,' said Neena, getting up with some difficulty.

'They don't shine so brightly,' I said. 'Fading stars, mostly.'

'You're just jealous. Wouldn't you like to be in films?'

'I'm not sure. There's something to be said for anonymity.'

She took me by the arm and we staggered around to the front of the house. They had given up shooting under trees (too hazardous) and were doing a scene on the lawn.

'They've trampled all over the flower beds,' said H.H. 'Not a chrysanthemum survives.'

Someone brought her a chair and she subsided into it. A young woman stepped out of the crowd, ran over to us, and touched Neena's feet.

'Somebody loves you,' I said.

'Everybody loves me.'

'And your rubies and your pearls.'

'Shut up, you impoverished hack.'

I shut up.

Nasha Naveen was doing a scene with the little starlet who had spoken to me on my arrival. I couldn't catch the dialogue, but he was promising her something and she was expressing her thanks; then her expression changed and she lunged forward, a dagger in her hand. It looked quite realistic. Nasha retreated, and in doing so, stepped all over H.H.'s snapdragons. Neena's reaction was equally realistic.

'Get out of my flower bed, you fat fool!' she

screamed. And rising from her chair, she made for him with a garden rake. Naveen fled the scene.

'Cut!' called the director. 'Take a break!'

As though on cue, half a dozen small dogs appeared from various directions, snapping, barking, hysterical in their determination to oust the intruders from H.H.'s premises. I didn't know there were so many; H.H. had been breeding both pekes and Poms.

Nasha Naveen hadn't gone far when an outraged Pom flew at his legs, ripping his trousers. He took refuge in the nearest make-up van. The camera crew scattered, while others took refuge in the makeshift canteen and the outhouses that had been placed at their disposal. Shooting was over for the day.

When the commotion had subsided and Hans had taken the dogs away, the producer joined H.H. and me for a quiet gin and tonic. Another gentleman was hovering around, waiting to be introduced, but nobody seemed to know him.

'Is he one of your people?' asked the producer.

'No,' said Neena. 'I thought he was with you.'

'I'm Koshi,' said the intruder. 'Just stopped by on a little business.'

'With me or with him?' asked H.H.

'With both of you, actually. How is the film going?'

'We're about halfway through. Next week we'll be shooting in Simla.'

'Excellent! Then perhaps there will be a small role for my daughter?'

'Your daughter! Who is she? Or rather, who are you?'

'I'm Koshi. Income tax inspector. You must be having to spend a lot of money locally—especially at this beautiful location. A real palace! All accounted for, I'm sure.'

'Sit down and have a drink,' said Neena cordially.

'Just nimbu-pani,' said the tax inspector, and sat down. 'My daughter's very talented, you know.'

'Give her a role,' said Neena. 'And see that she's well paid.'

'I'm sure we can find a small part for her,' said the producer. 'Can she dance?'

'No.'

'Can she sing?'

'No.'

'Has she done any acting?'

'No.'

'Perfect! We are looking for someone just like that.'

'Someone without any talent,' added H.H. 'How refreshing! She can start from scratch.'

'I'm sure she's good-looking,' said the producer anxiously.

'Looks a bit like me,' said Mr Koshi, smiling and exposing his gingivitis. 'I'll bring her along tomorrow.'

'Fine, fine,' said the producer. 'Have another nimbu-pani.'

'Tomorrow,' said Mr Koshi. 'And keep those accounts ready. No hurry, of course. But just in case . . .'

Mr Koshi made his departure, and for Neena's sake I was glad the dogs had been locked up. A wounded income tax inspector would have been hard to mollify.

'Be careful,' was Neena's warning to the producer. 'A man who drinks nothing but nimbu-pani can be very dangerous.'

18

Houses, like human beings, ultimately look dejected or cheerful according to their experience. Hollow Oak had been a lively, if not always a happy, sort of place during the Montalban era. I hadn't seen it during the Brigadier's brief tenure. During the filming of *Patloon* it still had a look of optimism, as though good things might yet be in store for its occupants. But after the film people had gone, the palace seemed to suffer from the depression that now took hold of Neena.

But it was not something that happened overnight; nor was it caused by any particular event or person. It was just that Neena had nothing to look forward to—apart from the whisky or vodka bottle.

But I am anticipating events. The producer did manage to complete his film, but *Patloon* flopped at the box office. After two more flops, the producer committed suicide; the director went on to win awards, but then fell foul of the Bollywood mafia. He was shot dead outside his Byculla house.

The tax inspector's daughter did quite well for herself in Mumbai—not as an actress, but as a fashion designer. Although not in the same class as one or two others, her costumes were in great demand, especially in monster movies. My old friend Pablo would have approved.

H.H. would not have approved of this diversion in my tale, as she always liked to be the centre of attention. A tragedy queen, if ever there was one. At times, she reminded me of Gloria Swanson in *Sunset Boulevard*.

I continued to see her, of course. Should old acquaintance be forgot and all that, and besides, I still felt a certain affection for her, a residue of loss from earlier times.

∾

My phone rang and I heard her familiar cackle at the other end. 'Come and see me, Ruskin, I'm dying.'

'You're dying for a drink, old girl.'

'Don't call me old girl. I'm still the Maharani of Mastipur.'

And so, feeling in need of a drink and her company, I'd go along to see her.

She was living alone, with Hans, the dogs and a couple of old retainers. Seema had long since returned to her home in Ranchi. The palace was beginning to crumble a little, like Miss Havisham's uncut wedding cake in *Great Expectations*. And on every visit, there seemed to be more dogs in the grounds.

The canine population had certainly multiplied. Poms had crossed with pekes, Samoyeds with dachshunds, and their progeny displayed the most amazing variety of shapes and sizes. One wing of the estate had been given up for them. They slept on old sofas, copulated on expensive rugs, defecated wherever it was convenient. Once a week Hans cleared their rooms out; no one else would undertake the task. Out of curiosity I once opened the door to one of these chambers and nearly passed out, the stink was so awful.

During the day the dogs had the run of the grounds. Although not fearsome to look at, they were aggressive and made a lot of noise, like street children from a slum. Prince Kartik sulked outside the gate, demanding money and making empty threats. Prince Karan drove by in his sports car; his curses and threats were more menacing, drug induced. Hans kept them at bay, but they were in no hurry—they knew that H.H. was not the terror of old.

Had there ever been much love between Neena and her boys? None of them seemed capable of it. They say blood is thicker than water, but I think there was more strontium than blood in their veins. Neena's early married years had been full of revelry, carefree abandon, self-gratification. The boys had been free to do as they pleased. Neither finished school, so confident were they of a future as wealthy young princes, even though they had long since been deprived of their titles. One day, Mummy's jewels would be theirs, Mummy's palace would be theirs, Mummy's bank accounts would be at their disposal. While she lived, she kept them on short rations, fixed allowances. They were always running into debt, then running to Mummy for help. She made them wait, watched them being humiliated. Prince Kartik, now in his late forties, was almost permanently intoxicated, and it was doubtful if he would outlive his mother. Stumbling home at night, he would often be waylaid by ruffians, robbed of the little money he carried. If he'd bought a bottle of rum in town, it would be taken from him. So he paid the taxi drivers to drop off his evening quota or quotas, and sometimes they would join him in a night's orgy of drinking. They would break up at dawn, and Kartik would sleep till noon, too comatose to get up to go to the bathroom, his mattress and bed sheets soaked in urine.

The younger brother stayed away most of the time, indulging in orgies of a different kind in the Mastipur palace. Women were brought to him; he played the prince, and spoke of great days to come. Like his father, he was fond of guns, although hunting was now prohibited. He always kept a revolver beside him, took potshots at domestic hens and inoffensive dogs and cats.

Neena blamed Sister Clarissa for their poor upbringing.

'Why Sister Clarissa?' I asked, on one of my visits, which were becoming increasingly rare.

She was propped up in bed, a glass of whisky on the bedside table, her favourite peke occupying the only chair. I sat at the foot of the bed—as far as I could get from the peke, who was rolling one eye at me in a sinister manner. It is said that after some time the owner of a pet dog begins to resemble the dog. In this case, I think the dog was beginning to resemble its owner. The peke was behaving like Neena—neurotic, selfish, arrogant.

'Does he drink too?' I asked.

'Who?'

'The peke?'

'He gets a teaspoon of brandy every night.'

'Lucky dog. But to return to Sister Clarissa: she wasn't a real nun, was she? And Dr Bisht wasn't even sure of her sex.'

'She wasn't a real nun, that's true. We kept her identity a secret. It was my husband's father, the great Maharaja, who brought her to India towards the end of the First World War. She was very young then, some say beautiful—but she was wanted by the French, by the British—you see, she'd been a German spy! So he smuggled her out of Europe dressed as a nun.'

'It sounds fantastic.'

'Those were fantastic times. And do you know who she was?'

'No.'

'Mata Hari.'

'Mata Hari! Not *the* Mata Hari. But she was executed—shot by a French firing squad.'

'That's what the history books say. But she escaped. The great Maharaja was one of her lovers, and in those days the Maharajas were powerful people. They had immense wealth, they ruled over millions—he had a lot of influence everywhere. He brought Mata Hari to India. But India was British India then, and Britain was at war with Germany. Had she been caught here, she might well have been shot.

'So she kept her disguise—remained at the Maharaja's court, looked after his affairs, helped

159

in bringing up my husband. And before the great Maharaja died, he made my husband promise to take care of her. Which he did, of course. After all, she'd been his nanny.'

'So much for the history books,' I said, and helped myself to more whisky. It seemed an incredible story, and yet it could have been true. Even during World War II, German citizens living in India had been rounded up and kept in detention camps. The largest of these camps was in Dehra Dun. Many of those detained were Nazis, among them Heinrich Harrer, who managed to escape to Tibet. All this had happened while I was a boy in Dehra.

'If Mata Hari was a German, how did she get such a name?'

'It wasn't her real name, silly. Her father was Dutch, her mother Javanese. She became famous as a dancer all over Europe, and her stage name was Mata Hari. In Javanese that means Eye of the Morning.'

'And was she still beautiful when you first saw her?'

'She was well over forty when I married the young Maharaja. Remember, the first Rani committed suicide.'

160

'Yes, I've heard about that.' And I remembered my mother and her friend Doreen talking about the mysterious circumstances surrounding the first Maharani's death, and their belief that it had been murder and that the nun had something to do with it.

'She was very loyal to your family, wasn't she?'

'Oh, she'd have done anything for them.'

'And she must have been very old when she died—when she fell down those stairs.'

'Must have been nearing ninety. Never told us her age.'

'Some say she wasn't a woman at all. That she was half a man—a hermaphrodite.'

'I wouldn't know. I always thought of her as a woman. Well, nuns usually are, aren't they? But then, the great Maharaja had strange tastes.'

'So did Count Dracula. It was normal to be abnormal. And your husband. All those rats.'

'Rats! Don't talk about rats. I hate them. They're all over the place!'

Her mood had changed. She'd enjoyed telling me about Sister Clarissa who was really Mata Hari; but her husband's hobby was anathema to her, which was natural enough, if indeed he had been consumed, literally, by his hobby.

'You can go now,' she said, bringing my visit to an abrupt end. 'I'm tired. We'll talk another day. And on your way out, tell Hans to bring me a hot-water bottle. It's cold in here. And don't kick the dogs.'

'Even if they bite me?'

'I *hope* they bite you. Now go. I want to be alone.'

'Garbo in *Grand Hotel*,' I said, by way of a parting shot.

'What's that?'

'Greta Garbo. Her famous line: *I want to be alone*.'

'Not Greta Garbo, Mata Hari,' she murmured, and fell asleep.

19

On a frosty December morning the phone rang, getting me out of a warm bed. Most days the phone was out of order; but sometimes it would come to life in the middle of the night, and then it would be a wrong number. On one occasion a ghostly voice said, 'There's a bomb in the dicky of your car.' This didn't worry me, as I don't have a car. Just a prankster, assuming everyone has a car.

It was Hans on the line. 'Maharani Sahiba wants to see you. She isn't too well.'

'I'll come over in the evening.'

'She says it's urgent. Wants you to witness her will.'

'I've already witnessed several wills. In the last one she left everything to some godman in Mauritius.'

'Well, she's changed her mind again, it seems. Maybe it's you, sir.'

'In that case I wouldn't be a witness. I'll be there in an hour or two. Hope you're the lucky one.'

I found Neena in bed, a place where she'd spent a lot of time, for one reason or another. Usually it was for pleasure; now it was pain.

'I think my kidneys have gone,' she said. 'I'm passing blood with my urine.'

'Have you seen Dr Bisht?'

'He came over yesterday. Said I should get admitted to the hospital. But I don't want to die in hospital.'

'You don't want to die at all,' I said. 'And you're looking fine.' This wasn't true. She was looking haggard. Her cheeks had fallen in, there were dark circles under her eyes, and her lips were dry and colourless. I was no doctor, but I could see that she was really ill.

'Kings and queens should die in their palaces,' she said. 'But this one is full of rats.'

'Rats? I haven't seen any rats. Not with so many dogs about the place.'

'They're not afraid of the dogs. They're big rats. And some are white. And some are black and white.'

'I haven't seen any.' I thought perhaps she was imagining things, hallucinating.

'They're the descendants of my husband's rats. Must have been lurking and breeding here for years . . . And now they are coming for me. I want you to get rid of them. That's why I sent for you.'

'Hans would do a better job of killing rats. But I haven't seen any.'

'You have to chase them away. You're Peter Pan, remember.'

'No, the Pied Piper. And he had a flute.'

'He played on his flute, and the rats ran after him.'

'Well, they're not running after me. You go to sleep and I'll look around and see if I can find any rats.'

But she had no intention of sleeping. For a while she forgot about rats. Something else was on her mind.

'Bring me my jewel case.'

'Where is it?'

'Bottom drawer of my dresser. The key's in that flowerpot.'

'There are three flowerpots. One has a geranium

growing in it. The other contains a croton. I don't know what's in the third.'

'It's a Christmas cactus, stupid. The key is in the cactus.'

'And Christmas is coming,' I said, getting my finger and thumb scratched as I found the key. I opened the bottom drawer of the dresser and found a walnut-wood case, about the size of a shoebox.

'You should have kept this in a bank locker,' I said.

'I like to look at my jewels. I can't go to the bank every day in order to gloat over them.'

'Well then, gloat,' I said, handing her the box. 'It might help you to get better. When I was a small boy I used to feel good looking at my marbles. I had a biscuit tin full of marbles. Very pretty marbles too. But it's a long time since I saw kids playing marbles.'

'They don't play with marbles any more. They play video games. Loss of innocence.'

'I don't think we were ever innocent.'

She took the jewel case from me. 'Now where's the key to the box?'

'In the Christmas cactus?'

'No, the other one, under the croton leaf.'

'If I were the geranium, I'd feel left out.'

'Don't be facetious. Give me the key.'

She opened the box, tilted it, and out tumbled a shower of gemstones. Just like marbles, only prettier. There were rubies and pearls, garnets and opals, an emerald set in a ring, a diamond bracelet, and a few other gems which I couldn't recognize.

'The emerald ring was my husband's,' said Neena. 'It was his birthstone. He was born in May.'

'So was I,' I said.

'Well, you can't have it.'

'I'm a staunch Taurean.'

'Then get your own emerald.'

'I'll settle for a couple of pearls.'

'Stop joking, and help me count. I have to make an inventory.'

'An inventory? What on earth for? You're not giving them away. I've never known you to give anything away, although you did once offer me your late husband's dress coat.'

'You can still have it.'

'No thanks. Give it to Hans. It will fit him better.'

'I'm giving him the house. And the dogs.'

'He has to feed the dogs.'

'He'll get some money. I have to decide about

the jewels. There are those useless sons of mine. And there are cousins and aunts and nephews. Now help me count.'

Twenty minutes later we had made a list of the contents of the jewel box. It then went back into the bottom drawer of the dresser. One key went into the Christmas cactus, and just for fun I gave the second key to the geranium. Neena didn't notice. She was staring at something that was moving about in a dark corner of the bedroom, not far from the door.

'It's a rat,' she said. 'There's a rat in here.'

I went to the door and opened it, and the little peke ran in and jumped on the bed.

'No rat,' I said. 'Just your ratty little dog.'

'Go away,' she said. 'There's nothing in my will for you.' She burst into a fit of hysterical laughter.

'The trouble with you, dear Ruskin, is that you're too bloody happy. I hate people who are happy. You don't care if you succeed or not. You're a hippy disguised as a man of the world. You're one of life's failures. And that's why I'm quite fond of you.'

'Well, having come all this way to see you in spite of your nasty dogs, I must be fond of you too.'

And we both broke down laughing.

20

There were rats at Hollow Oak.

Hans phoned to say that they were all over the place and that H.H. was getting quite hysterical. Dr Bisht came to see her every day. But she wouldn't get out of bed and go to hospital.

'Phone the municipality,' I said. 'Get hold of the executive officer. Ask him to send some people over to catch or kill the rats.'

'I've already done so—they sent us their dog-catchers instead. H.H. was very upset.'

'I'll come over with some rat poison,' I said.

Ruskin Bond

'Don't do that. The dogs might consume it.'

I didn't go over that day. In spite of being the failure that Neena loved, I did get the occasional writing assignment and I had an article to finish.

In December, the sunset stretched right across the horizon, a river of molten light, changing from marigold to pomegranate red to crimson. Before it set, the sun threw a shaft of golden light across my study wall, and there, for the first time, I thought I saw the face, or rather the profile, of my old friend Pablo—or rather my young friend Pablo, for there was no change in his features—and he smiled briefly in my direction before fading with the dying sun.

A message, a premonition? Or just a whisper of lost friendship. The world is smaller than we think. We are all parts of one another, meeting, separating, meeting again, looking for our severed halves, heedless of time and distance . . .

∽

Next day the phone rang again, and Hans said, rather dramatically, 'She's been bitten.'

'By one of the dogs?'

'No, by a rat. And her favourite peke is missing. She's hysterical.'

When I arrived at Hollow Oak the gate was open and some of the dogs were on the road. For once they did not bark at me. As I approached the front steps, a huge rat, about two feet long, darted out of the open doorway and disappeared into the bushes.

Seconds later, it was followed by another.

These were no ordinary rats; these were huge field rats, seldom seen in the town.

Dr Bisht was in the bedroom, examining Neena. For once she was silent. Her limbs were in a clonic condition, relaxing and contracting in rapid succession.

'She's had a shock,' said the doctor. 'There's more than one bite.'

Blood was trickling down one of her arms.

'It seems a big bite.'

'I've injected her with a sedative,' he said. 'She's calmer but her muscles keep contracting.'

'Before you came, she had several convulsions,' said Hans.

'Could it be tetanus,' I ventured.

'I'm not sure, but I've given her a tetanus shot.'

'Could it be rabies?'

'Too early for that. But we can't leave her here. We must get her to the hospital whether she likes it or not.'

I left the room and phoned for the local ambulance. It took about an hour to arrive, and by then, Neena was out of this world.

21

Death holds life together. Once we lose our fear of death, something happens to life. It is this fear that keeps us on our toes, keeps us going, makes us savour the joy of being alive. Those who are near to death fear it not so much as those who are in the fullness of health and the enjoyment of life. They are conscious of what they have to lose. And for H.H., the contemplation of oblivion, of nothingness, had always been frightful.

Life, for Neena, had been one long party, and so she had been frightened at the very end. Now the next stage of her journey had begun—if, indeed, there is a next stage . . .

The immediate and unavoidable journey involved a drive down to the cremation ground in Dehra. An obliging taxi driver helped us to place the body on the roof of his car, where it was firmly strapped down. Dr Bisht, Hans and I sat in the car. H.H.'s servants followed in a bus. Hardly a royal procession!

The people at the cremation ground were well-practised and efficient, and it did not take long for our Maharani's mortal remains to be consumed by the purifying and liberating flames of the pyre.

As we stood there respectfully (Neena would have laughed to see our sombre faces), contemplating our own inevitable dissolution, I asked the good doctor, 'What did she really die of?'

'She died of fright, I think.'

'Is that what you put on the death certificate?'

'No, I don't think that would have been acceptable. I just wrote Respiratory Failure.'

'That covers everything, I suppose.'

The funeral was almost over when Prince Kartik turned up, quite drunk of course, proclaiming that he would be immolated beside his mother.

To everyone's embarrassment, he went to the wrong funeral pyre, flinging wreaths and garlands of marigold on the smouldering remains of a poor and friendless woman of the streets.

Hollow Oak had been left unattended, and in our absence thieves had broken into the house and ransacked most of the rooms. The drawer of Neena's dresser had been forced open, its contents strewn about. The jewel box was missing.

∾

At first I thought Prince Karan had something to do with the break-in, but we learnt later that he was in Mastipur at the time of his mother's death. Even so, the robbery could have been perpetrated by his associates, a sinister band of layabouts who would stop at nothing in the pursuit of wine, women and money.

There were various claimants to the property. Both the sons contested Neena's last will, claiming that she was of unsound mind when she made it. The same claim could have been made for most of her earlier wills. At least two religious ashrams laid claim to the property, as did a son from the first Maharani, who turned up unexpectedly and asserted that he was the true heir to the late Maharaja's estate. It was a claim that had to be taken seriously.

Our system of justice is slow and frustrating at the best of times. In a case where there were so many claims and counterclaims, it would take years for a conclusion to be reached. Prince Kartik was already on his last legs; he wouldn't see the coming spring. Prince Karan had possession of the Mastipur palace. His debauchery and drug dealing had made him many enemies, and they would catch up with him sooner or later.

Meanwhile, Hans and the dogs occupied Hollow Oak, but the loyal Swiss was having a hard time of it. His funds were limited, and feeding the dogs was a problem. The rats, bolder and bigger than ever, were helping themselves to most of the rations. Veg or non-veg, they weren't fussy.

The servants, unpaid, drifted away. The buildings suffered from lack of maintenance. Roofs began to leak, walls became damp and grimy. A house in the hills, if unoccupied and unattended even for a few months, begins to disintegrate. Every time I passed

Hollow Oak, it looked shabbier than before. You could run or jump all over the flower beds; there were no flowers to destroy. No music, no laughter issued from its doors and windows. Most of them were shut. Here and there, an unloved dog roamed about the grounds.

Unloved, that was the best way to describe the palace and its occupants.

And who would remember H.H.? Well, I would for some time. I still do. Can't forget her. And so perhaps would the Montalbans, in whatever distant land they happened to be. Ricardo certainly. And Mr Lobo, as he strums out *As time goes by* on some hotel's grand piano. And Hans?

Well, after a few months he couldn't stand the loneliness and isolation. He was hard up, too. So he packed a bag and took off, never to be seen again in Mussoorie. Someone spotted him in Kathmandu, acting as a sort of guide for European tourists travelling through Nepal.

The courts sent a receiver to seal the palace until all the lawsuits were settled. The dogs gradually disappeared, found new homes, or became strays. The rats went too, as they could hardly exist by eating the furniture. Some found havens in the kitchens of school and hotels.

~

I don't go that way any more. There's a footpath that bypasses Hollow Oak, and I use it on my walks to the town and home again. The cinemas have all shut down, but I walk to the bank and the post office and sometimes the local bookshops. Living on my own, I have become a fairly good cook.

The other evening, as the twilight faded swiftly and a nightjar began its evening recitation, I strolled down to the cottage, feeling a little low and wondering if I should just pack up and go away too.

Someone stood in the shadows.

A familiar figure. I recognized her instantly.

'Leela,' I said. 'What brings you here?'

'I'm hungry,' she said. 'And I have something for you.'

'And your sister?'

'She's on duty.'

I gazed at her with a certain affection. There she was, chubby and cheerful and uncomplicated.

'I've brought you something,' she said, handing me a parcel. 'Hans asked me to give it to you. Maharani Sahiba had told him it was to be given to you. He left it with us when he went away, but we didn't get a chance to see you.'

I took the parcel and placed it on the window seat.

'Sit down, Leela,' I said. 'I roasted a chicken today. You can share it with me.'

Leela helped me polish off the chicken. I took the empty dishes to the kitchen, and when I returned to the sitting room, she'd gone!

'Funny girl,' I said aloud, and gave my attention to the parcel.

It contained the late Maharaja's dress coat, or sherwani, the same one that H.H. had once tried to give me. It seemed that she'd been determined that I should have it. Nothing special about the coat. The buttons were just buttons, not made of rubies or pearls. But a handsome coat, meant for a handsome man. Perhaps that was the message; that I was worthy of a maharaja's dress coat. Or had she just been teasing me again?

I wasn't going to wear it, but I put it away carefully. It would be a reminder of the good times had by all of us—H.H., Ricardo, Mrs Montalban, Pablo and Anna, Mr Lobo, myself. And if, at the end, the times weren't so good, it was probably because the party had gone on for too long.

Classic
Ruskin Bond

Complete and Unabridged

The Room on the Roof, Vagrants in the Valley, Delhi Is Not Far, A Flight of Pigeons, The Sensualist, A Handful of Nuts

The Fiction Omnibus:

This collection of six novels sparkles with the quiet charm and humanity that are the hallmarks of Ruskin Bond's writing. Evoking nostalgia for a time gone by, these poignant chronicles of life in India's hills and small towns describe the hopes and passions that capture young minds and hearts, highlighting the uneasy reconciliation of dreams and destiny.

'One of the best storytellers of contemporary India'
—*Tribune*

Classic
Ruskin Bond Volume 2

The Memoirs

*Rain in the Mountains, Scenes from a Writer's Life, The
Lamp Is Lit, Landour Days, Notes from a Small Room*

The Non-fiction Omnibus:

This volume brings together Ruskin Bond's autobiographical
writings—memoirs, essays, journals, philosophical musings—
of over five decades. As Bond writes about the experiences of
his formative years that came to shape his art, of life's little
joys and fleeting regrets, of the eccentricities of friends and
family, of the birds and flowers that each season brings, he
transports us to a more elegant world where time moves at
a gentler pace. Brimming over with his trademark wisdom,
warmth and candour, this collection shows why Ruskin Bond
is one of India's most treasured writers.

'Our very own resident Wordsworth in prose'
—*India Today*